Web of Conspiracy

Book Three

Tarnished Valor

By

Herbert Grosshans

Published by
Melange Books, LLC
White Bear Lake, MN 55110
www.melange-books.com

Web of Conspiracy, Book Three, Tarnished Valor
By Herbert Grosshans, Copyright © 2011

ISBN: 978-1-61235-026-4

Credits
Copy Editor: Sherry Derr Wille
Line Editor: Mae Powers
Format Editor: Mae Powers
Cover Artist: A.Bratt

Web of Conspiracy
Book Three: Tarnished Valor
By Herbert Grosshans

A decision Jeff Chartrand made in Iraq has serious consequences. A friend rescues him and he has a torrid love affair. News of another murder makes his world come crashing down. He and his team uncover a plot within the US to assassinate the President and it becomes a race against time to foil the plans of a terrorist group.

Visit Herbert's website:

http://hegro.shawwebspace.ca
http://hegro.blogspot.com/

Works also by and including Herbert Grosshans at
www.melange-books.com:
Stars In Chains 1, Slave
Stars In Chains 2: Liberator
Stardogs 1 & 2
The Xandra Trilogy
Cliffs of Time
Orion the Hunt
Beyond the Stars Digest
Orion: Symbiont of Passion
Men of Eros
Web of Conspiracy, Book 1& 2
The Spider Wars Series

Prologue

When Detective Jeff Chartrand and his partner Maxine Montana are sent to investigate a shooting, he finds his brother Michael, his sister-in-law Samantha, and his nephew Joseph murdered. Victims of a drug deal gone wrong, according to Detective Sheppard, but Jeff does not believe it. He is taken off the case for personal reasons. When they find evidence that Michael might have had connections to Joseph Galliano, a known mobster, Jeff decides to look up Galliano. According to Galliano, Michael owes him five thousand dollars, money he lost gambling. Galliano wants his money, but Jeff tells him he has to wait for it.

Michael Chartrand was a decorated war hero. He served in Iraq, where he was a member of a unit they called the *Ten Commandos*. When Jeff tries to contact one of Michael's war buddies, he finds that he and his wife have been shot to death in their apartment. Another one, Dennis Kim, lies in a Fresno hospital, in a coma, after someone beat him up in an apparent botched robbery. Jeff drives to Fresno and meets Connie Wu, Kim's roommate. She shows him pictures of the soldiers who were the *Ten Commandos*.

One of men in the pictures, Ronald Larkin, the CO of the unit, is now running for Senator, but his ultimate goal is to become President of the United States. Connie believes that the two murders and the attack on her friend Dennis are connected. She suspects that Ronald Larkin's life might be in danger. Jeff and Connie feel an attraction for each other and before Jeff drives home, he and Connie make love. She is the first woman he has been intimate with since his wife's death.

Among Michael's belongings Jeff finds a key to a safety deposit box, part of a journal, and an envelope with some photos of a dark haired girl holding a baby. He also discovers that Michael sent two hundred dollars every month to Iraq through the local mosque.

Jeff and Montana go to one of Larkin's campaigns and try to tell him he might be next on the list, but Larkin is not worried. "I have a good bodyguard in John Parker. He keeps me safe." John Parker is one of the *Ten Commandos*. Larkin shows an interest in Michael's journal and he wants to know if there are any pictures or other stuff from Iraq.

When Jeff and Montana drive home, she tells him she wants him to make love to her. He has never thought of her as a woman before, just his partner, but suddenly he finds her quite attractive and he takes her home to his apartment. She spends the night with him.

A few days later, when Jeff and Montana come home from a dinner, a man by the name of Ethan Grey tries to shoot him and Jeff kills him in self-defense. Ethan Grey is another former member of the *Ten Commandos*. He has with him an attaché case with pictures of Jeff and the other members of the unit. It seems, Ethan Grey was the assassin, but Jeff is not convinced.

When Jeff arrives at the precinct after the shootout, he is interviewed by two agents from Homeland Security. Agent Dave MacKay and Agent Manning. They are accusing him of having ties to the Muslim community and to Al Queda. They show him a printout of a bank account with his and Michael's name on it. There are over hundred thousand dollars on the account. Jeff has no idea that account existed, but the agents don't believe him. Dave MacKay is the twin brother of John MacKay, who was also a member of the *Ten Commandos*. He apparently died by friendly fire in Iraq, just like Darrin Montana, Maxine's brother.

Internal Affairs suspends Jeff. He tells Maxine (Montana) about his time in the army, tells her he was a member of Grey Ops, a special unit in Army Intelligence, and that he is contemplating going back to his old unit. Jeff finds an SD card in a safety box belonging to his brother. On it are disturbing images. Pictures of American soldiers helping Iraqis unloading boxes from US Military vehicles. There is even a small video depicting the rape of an Iraqi girl and her murder by American soldiers.

While visiting his sister, Jeff meets Werner Reinhart, a German. Reinhart is an old friend of Jeff's brother-in-law. Jeff has misgivings about the jovial German, who comes across like a friendly, charming gentleman. It turns out that Reinhart is a mercenary and he seems to remember Michael from Iraq.

Jeff drives back to Fresno to talk to a Detective Smith, who has shown an interest in Jeff's problem. He finds out that Dennis Kim has been shot to death in his hospital bed. He spends the night with Connie. He promises her to be back for the funeral.

After arriving home, he finds a message on his answering machine asking him to meet with Colonel Cowley, his former commander. Cowley asks Jeff to join the unit again. Only then will he be able to help him with his search for his brother's murderer.

That same day, he meets a woman, who introduces herself as Kalila Ahmed. She tells him she is the sister of the girl in the photos Jeff found among Michael's possessions. The little baby is Michael's son. His name is Omar. She also tells him her sister has been stoned to death by the people in her village, because she committed an unforgivable sin. Omar is now in an orphanage.

Jeff also meets two Iraqi men, who want back the twenty thousand dollars they deposited in Michael's account before he was murdered. He tells them he knows nothing about the money. The men warn him that things might get ugly if they don't get their money back.

In the meantime, Galliano has been phoning Jeff's sister demanding the five thousand dollars, except now he wants thirty thousand. Jeff pays him another visit. During the confrontation, he kills Galliano and his body guard Tony Moretti. He is arrested for the murder and taken into custody. One of the arresting officers is Maxine Montana.

Elias Morgan, an attorney, gets Jeff out of jail. Morgan reveals he has been with Grey Ops since its conception and he knows everything about Jeff. Jeff is hiding out in a safe house owned by the Military.

A group that calls itself *The Needle of Allah* kidnaps Omar, Michael's son. Colonel Cowley sends Jeff and his new team to Iraq to rescue the little boy. Accompanying him are Cowley's son Rob Masters and Kalila, the Iraqi woman who claimed to be Omar's aunt. She works for Iraqi Intelligence and came to America to stop the selling of arms to insurgents.

In Iraq, after following a wrong lead, Jeff, Kalila, and Sergeant Abduk are taken prisoner by insurgents. They manage to escape, but Abduk is wounded and needs medical attention. Lost in the marshlands south of Baghdad, they receive help from the Ma'dan, the Marsh Arabs, who hate the insurgents.

Following a new lead and with the help of satellite surveillance photos, the location of the insurgent group *The Needle of Allah* is discovered and the team travels to Al Kut and rescues Omar. Jeff has no mercy with the kidnappers and the team kills them all.

Jeff's suspicion that rescuing Omar was not the whole reason Colonel Cowley sent the team to Iraq proves correct when he receives new orders. His mission: Prevent the delivery of arms to another group of insurgents.

Jeff and his men travel toward the Iranian border. They overcome the insurgents and take over the base. When the trucks arrive at the base to deliver the weapons, a short battle ensues and Jeff's team takes the accompanying mercenaries prisoner. Angry about American soldiers betraying their country, Jeff has one of them, Lieutenant George Stiller, executed.

Among the mercenaries is a man Jeff knows. Werner Reinhart, the German he met at his sister's house. Jeff makes a deal with the man…his freedom for information about the people who are behind the selling of illegal arms.

Kalila is critically wounded during the battle and the team rushes back to the military base in Baghdad. Jeff pleads with the commander of the base to send Kalila to a hospital in Germany. His feelings for Kalila are more than just friendship, but he knows that she is unattainable for him because of their different backgrounds and religions.

The team flies back to the US. After arriving at the military base in Sacramento, Jeff and the team are taken into custody. They are told that Colonel Cowley has been relieved of his post and a Colonel O'Connor has assumed Cowley's position.

O'Connor does not recognize Jeff as a soldier. As far as he is concerned, Jeff is a civilian and he wants to hand him over to the local police. Rob and some of the others smuggle Jeff off the base and take him back to the safe house, where Rob colors Jeff's hair and beard red and provides him with a false passport. Jeff Chartrand is now Dr. Richard Raymond Callwell, a chiropractor from Canada. On holiday in the US.

Werner Reinhart had lied to Jeff about being able to tell him details about the people he worked for, but he does provide enough information for Jeff to follow up on. He and Rob fly to Dallas to talk to Mike Black who runs Private Guards and Protection Agency. He doesn't know who sends him the orders to hire mercenaries. After leaning on Black, Jeff gets some information, but not as much as he had hoped for.

They fly back home and Jeff visits Connie in Fresno and he spends a few days with her. He realizes that he has fallen in love with Connie. Before he leaves her, she gives him an envelope, which was given to her by Brian McGee, one of Michael's war buddies. The envelope is to be opened should something happen to him. It contains information that might point to his killers. Jeff gives the envelope to Morgan for safekeeping.

Back in Sacramento, he calls his sister Barbara, who tells him that a man with a heavy accent phoned and wanted to know where he could find Jeff. She also tells him that Michael's former boss called and told her that he has a flash drive that belongs to Michael. Jeff drives to Michael's shop and picks up the flash drive. Later, he meets with Maxine in a hotel and they have sex.

Jeff is beginning to have doubts about many things in his life. He questions the war in Iraq, religion, and his sudden feelings for Connie, Maxine, and for Kalila.

The information Rob gained from Black's computer points to Chicago, where the e-mails came from. Jeff and Rob fly to Chicago. Jeff has a new disguise. His name now is Jerry Hammer. He wears a wig with a ponytail.

After talking to a girl at Moore's Exotic Exports, they visit Nova Investments, where they interview her boyfriend Jimmy Marco, who admits that he sent the e-mails, but his orders come from his boss Benny Hardini. When they confront Hardini, he denies his involvement in the hiring of mercenaries.

Jeff phones his detective friend, Marvin Smith, in Fresno, and he finds out that Benny Hardini has a brother, Terrence Hardini, who works for Anthony Mariano, the Godfather of one of the Chicago mob families. Jeff also finds out that Joseph Galliano, the man he shot, was Mariano's cousin. Mariano is the owner of Banco Mariano. Jeff decides to pay the man a visit. They manage to get an appointment with Mariano. They tell him that they are interested in taking over Galliano's operation. During their conversation, Jeff finds out that Galliano had his brother Michael assassinated, after getting the orders from Mariano. Jeff wonders what possible connection Michael could have had with Mariano.

They find Jimmy Marco murdered and manage to get back into Benny Hardini's office, where they download files from his computer. On the way back to their hotel, an attempt is made on their life and during the shootout Jeff kills one of the assassins. His name is Terrence Hardini. Jeff knows Mariano put out the hit and they decide to go back to confront him.

Chapter One

When Jeff Chartrand and Rob Masters walked into Banco Mariano, they were happy to see that Leslie was not at his post behind the information desk. Heading for the elevators, they walked briskly but slow enough not to attract attention.

They took the public elevator up to the sixteenth floor and used the stairs to get back down to the fourteenth floor. Before they reached the fourteenth floor, Rob handed Jeff a pair of gloves. Jeff put them on without asking questions.

Walking silently across the plush carpet of the corridor, the expected two burly guards made their appearance, blocking their way.

"Hi, Jordan," Rob said. "How's life treating you these days?"

"What the fuck is it to you, faggot?" Jordan took a step toward Rob.

"Just making friendly conversation." He walked calmly up to the big man and kicked him in the crotch. Hard.

Jordan let out a surprised shout and bent forward, presenting his fat neck. Rob hit him with the edge of his hand and the big man fell like a dead tree.

Taken by surprise, the other guard went for his gun, but Jeff reached him before he could free it from its holster under his arm. His fist hit the man square on the chin and he went down.

"That part was easy." Rob chuckled. He bent to relieve Jordan of his weapon. Jeff did the same with the other man. Then they tied them up with the roll of tape they had brought.

"Time to enter the snake's den," Rob said, waving Jeff on. "After you, fearless leader."

Mariano's secretary gave them a friendly smile when they walked into the small front office. "Is Mr. Mariano in?" Jeff asked.

"Yes, he is, but I'm afraid he won't be able to see you. He's getting ready for a meeting with the mayor."

"That's okay," Rob said. Then he walked by her toward the door that led into Mariano's office.

"You can't go in there, sir," she called out.

"Don't worry," Jeff told her. "We won't be long."

Distracted by Rob, she hadn't been aware of Jeff coming closer and stepping behind the desk. He put his hand over her mouth and whispered, "Don't struggle and you won't get hurt." Then he taped her mouth shut and tied her hands behind her back. Wrapping a piece of tape around her ankles, he bound her against the chair.

In the meantime, Rob had gone back into the corridor and dragged in the two unconscious guards. He waited for Jeff by the door to Mariano's office until Jeff was finished with the secretary.

Mariano looked up when the door opened. He was just a silhouette inside his cloud of blue smoke. Jeff and Rob walked briskly toward his desk.

"What the hell!" Mariano cursed.

"Surprised to see us?" Rob asked the obese man. Then he pulled out his gun and pointed it at him. "Don't even think about getting your gun, Mr. Mariano. You'll never reach it in time."

"What's the meaning of this?" Mariano's wheezing voice sounded rough. If he was scared, he didn't show it.

"Why did you send your goons after us?" Jeff asked.

"I don't know what you're talking about."

"Really?" Jeff pulled the wallets out of his pocket, took out the driver's licenses and threw them onto the desk. "Have a look at these. Do these guys look familiar to you?"

Mariano glanced at the pictures. "Never seen them in my life."

"Don't lie. We know that Terrence Hardini works for you. "By the way, he's dead. Maybe you should arrange for his funeral."

Mariano glared at them from behind his oversized red-framed glasses. He looked like an owl eyeing a potential meal. "You two clowns are dead meat. How dare you come into my office and threaten me with a gun? What happened to my bodyguards?"

"They've decided to take some time off," Jeff said. "Last I seen them they were sleeping."

"Who the fuck are you? I've made some calls to Sacramento. They've never heard of you."

"That's because we don't exist." Rob grinned. "We're just a couple of clowns you'll wish you had never met."

"What do you want?"

"Justice," Jeff said.

Mariano managed to laugh. "Justice? What the fuck are you talking about?"

"I want you to tell me why you put out a hit on Michael Chartrand and his family?"

"Why? What's your interest in that?" Mariano wiped his face with a meaty hand. The first sign that he was becoming nervous.

"Michael Chartrand was my brother," Jeff said, his voice suddenly hoarse, the urge to put a bullet between the fat man's eyes stronger than ever. He restrained himself, knowing his time would come.

"Your brother?" Mariano wiped his face again. Jeff was close enough to see that the hand was shaking. The owl-eyes stared at him. "I thought your name was Harper."

"No. My name is Jeff Chartrand."

"That means you're that renegade cop who shot Galliano?"

"Congratulations. You're the winner of the quiz. Unfortunately, we can only give you the boo-boo prize."

"Which means?"

"A bullet in the head." Jeff smiled evilly. Any mercy or remorse he felt when they entered Mariano's office had vanished. There was nothing but coldness inside him. Coldness he hadn't experienced for sixteen years.

This was just another job that needed to be done.

"You can't murder me in cold blood!" Mariano protested. He tried to get up from his chair, but Rob waved his gun. "Stay put or you'll die right now!" His voice sounded chilly and crisp, showing no emotion.

Maybe Mariano saw a glimmer of hope in Rob's words. "I don't believe you'd be stupid enough and shoot me in my office. There are surveillance cameras everywhere. You were seen entering the building."

"That may be so, but I don't see any cameras in here," Rob said.

"They're hidden." Mariano spoke with a belligerent voice.

Rob chuckled. "I would have spotted them by now. Besides, you told us yourself we can speak freely in this room."

"Why did you have my brother killed?" Jeff injected softly.

"It wasn't my idea and I don't know the reason it was done. I didn't even know him." Mariano spread his fingers. "It was just business. Nothing personal at all."

"Just business?" Jeff roared. "You wipe out a whole family and you say it's just business?" He pulled out the gun he had taken from one of the bodyguards, took off the safety and walked up to Mariano. Putting

11

the gun against the man's head, he said with a calm, cold voice, "Well, this is not just business. This is highly personal."

Mariano sat frozen in his chair, staring up at Jeff, like a man in a trance. Then he seemed to come out of it. His hand shot out, reached for one of the drawers under the desk.

Jeff squeezed the trigger before Mariano's hand touched the drawer.

The sound of the gunshot was muffled by the closeness of the target but loud enough to shatter the silence in the room. The back of Mariano's head exploded and sprayed blood and brain matter over the chair and desk.

Jeff put his foot against the man's chest and gave it a push. The chair tipped backward and the gross body of the man who apparently was the Godfather of Chicago's mob sprawled onto the carpet, staining it red with blood.

"Fat pig!" Jeff cursed. He threw the gun on top of the body. Then he turned to look at Rob. "It's done," he said with a low, emotionless voice.

"Not quite," Rob said. He pulled a flash drive out of his pocket and connected it to Mariano's computer.

"We should get out of here," Jeff said.

"This won't take long." Rob proceeded with the download.

The secretary struggled in her chair when they came out of the office.

"Better cancel the meeting with the mayor," Rob told her. "I'm afraid Mr. Mariano won't be able to make it." He winked. "If anyone asks, tell them Dan Leighton from Sacramento sends his regards. Remember the name…Dan Leighton."

This time they took the private elevator down to the main floor and walked out of the building unmolested.

"We don't have much time," Rob said. "I figure we have about an hour. Enough time to enter the next phase of our operation and cover our tracks."

They stopped at a clothing store and Rob purchased some clothing, a duffle bag, and a gym bag. Then they drove to another department store, where Rob went into the public washroom to change. When he came back to the car, he had removed his thick mustache and was wearing a pair of glasses. He was dressed in a casual suit and wore a sporty cap on his head.

Jeff was happy to see the rings gone from his ears, finding Rob looking much more like a serious professional and not some playboy with nothing but straw between his ring-adorned ears.

They drove to the Holiday Inn. Jeff went up to the suite, while Rob checked into the hotel under the name Robert Cameron.

Jeff waited for Rob to join him in their old suite. Rob changed back into his original disguise and went down to the lobby to check out Mr. Roberts and Mr. Hammer.

Meanwhile, Jeff moved their stuff into the new room. It was smaller than the other one. They had only one room this time with two double beds, but it didn't matter. They'd be checking out before evening.

Rob knocked on the door half an hour later as his new persona Robert Cameron. "Time to change you back to Dr. Richard Callwell, Chiropractor from Canada," he said.

Jeff gladly removed the wig with the ponytail. Rob dyed his hair red again and glued a small piece of false beard on his bare strip of chin. Then Jeff exchanged his dark suite for a gray one.

They stuffed their old clothing and anything that might betray them into a large plastic bag. "We'll lose it on our way to the airport," Rob said.

They left the hotel at four o'clock, drove a few blocks and parked the rental car in a back lane. Then they threw the plastic bag and their suitcases into a dumpster. Looking for some garbage cans, they found a couple and deposited the dye and Jeff's wig into one of the cans.

Leaving the back lane, Jeff carried a duffle bag and Rob a gym bag. They hailed a cab and proceeded on their way to the airport.

"Looks like you two gentlemen are taking a trip," the cabbie said.

"Yeah, flying home again," Rob said.

"Where you from?"

"Dallas, Texas." Rob spoke suddenly with a Texas drawl.

"Never been there." The driver chuckled. "Never been anywhere. Born in Chicago, probably die in Chicago."

"I guess it's as good a place to die as any," Jeff said.

"Speaking of dying. Someone whacked Anthony Mariano." The cabbie spoke with a conspiratorial tone as if implying everyone knew who Anthony Mariano was.

"No kidden? Who's Anthony Mariano?" Rob asked.

"I'm surprised you never heard of him. He owns Banco Mariano." The driver turned his head to glance at them. "Word in the street is Mariano was the Godfather of one of the Mob families."

"Really? Do they know who…umm…whacked him?"

The cabbie shrugged. "The cops don't talk. If you ask me, it's somebody from outside. New York maybe. I just come from the airport. Lots of cops there. They'll probably close down the airport."

"I hope not," Jeff said. "I'd like to get home to my kids. These conventions sure take a lot out of you."

"Take my advice." The cabbie suggested, dropping his voice to a confidential level. "Don't try to smuggle anything on the plane. They'll be checking every piece of luggage, looking mainly for guns and ammunition."

"Good advice," Rob said in his new drawl. "But we don't have to worry. Guns scare the heck out of me. I don't touch 'em." He shook himself. "My daddy, may the Good Lord rest his soul, he was hunter and he always told me *Son, a man without a gun is not a man, it's the American way*, but after he nearly shot my younger brother while huntin' rattlers, my mamma gave him a piece of her mind. She was a feisty one, my ma. No, siri, I don't touch no gun."

"Well, if you'd live in Chicago you'd be singing a different tune. I've got one in my glove compartment. Just in case."

"You're a brave man. Ever use it?" Jeff asked.

"Hell no." The cabbie chuckled. "And I hope I'll never have to."

"Well, you know what the Good Book says. Those who live by the sword shall die by the sword. I'm aimin' to die a peaceful death. In my bed." Rob laughed loudly. "Some day in the far future, I hope. The Lord willin'."

"You sound just like one of those Evangelists on television," the cabbie said.

Rob chuckled. "Sometimes the Holy Spirit comes over me and I just have to shout the Good Word to my brothers and sisters. I'm a member of the Pentecostal Church. As a matter of fact, I feel like clappin' and dancin' right now. Hallelujah."

"Oh Lord," Jeff moaned beside him.

"Amen, my brother," Rob shouted, beaming. "Amen!"

"Well, here we are." The cabbie pulled up in front of the entrance to the airport. "Have a pleasant trip."

"Bless you, brother," Rob said.

Jeff waited until the cab pulled away, then he said, "I'm afraid to ask, but what the hell was the purpose of that little scene?"

"Creating an alibi in case he gets questioned, my brother. He won't remember much about us except the fact that we were two religious

14

men."

"I guess that can't hurt," Jeff agreed. "I'm always baffled how you so easily slip into these roles. You've missed your calling." He looked around and noticed the large number of police cars parked nearby. "What about our guns? What if they check your gym bag?"

"Don't worry. We won't be boarding any plane. We'll rent another car and drive to Indianapolis."

"You surprise me again, Rob. I was thinking the same thing."

They hailed another cab.

"Take us to the nearest rental car company," Rob told the driver.

Chapter Two

It was nearly midnight when they arrived in the outskirts of Indianapolis. They found a motel and booked two separate rooms.

Rob came into Jeff's room and said, "Turn on the TV. I'd like to see if Mariano made the national news already." He sat down on the bed and popped open a beer can. "That hamburger I had didn't agree with my stomach. I should have had those chicken fingers. Maybe a couple of beers will fix me up."

Jeff switched on the TV and joined Rob on the bed. After five minutes of commercials, the announcer appeared on the screen.

"The murder of well known Banker Anthony Mariano in Chicago has sent ripples through the stock market. The stocks of Banco Mariano dropped from two hundred and thirty dollars a share to one hundred ninety-seven and are expected to drop even further. A spokesman for the Chicago police says they have brought in the FBI. Even though they have a good description of the two men suspected of shooting Mariano, they don't have anyone in custody yet. The two men seem to have vanished without a trace. Police have released videos taken by surveillance cameras and we will broadcast them after the commercials. Stay tuned."

"They have videos," Rob said, chuckling. "Good luck."

"I'm glad we've decided against taking a plane in Chicago," Jeff said. "Even though we have changed our disguises, I wouldn't have felt comfortable, especially since I'm, according to my passport, not even a citizen of the US. They might scrutinize my passport and me a little closer."

"You have nothing to fear. That passport will pass inspection. My cousin Billy is the best forger I've ever met." Rob finished his beer and burped. "I'm feeling better already."

Jeff watched the video on the screen. It showed two men walking down a corridor. One of the men was big. He recognized himself, or to be more precise, his disguised persona. The other man was a little shorter

16

and not as bulky. Rob.

The angle shifted and then it showed them walking away from the camera. Jeff's false ponytail showed off prominently on his dark suit.

Seeing himself on the screen, he almost lifted his hand to touch the back of his head, but then he remembered he didn't have the ponytail anymore.

He watched the confrontation with Mariano's bodyguards and had to admit they handled the situation smoothly and with efficiency.

"We work well together," Rob said, voicing Jeff's own thoughts.

The video stopped and the announcer came back on. "Unfortunately, there were no cameras in Mr. Mariano's office and the actual murder was not recorded. There is a reward of ten thousand dollars for information leading to the arrest of the suspects. And now to local news…"

Jeff switched off the television. "I have to admit, the ponytail you made me wear was a stroke of genius, Rob, even though I hated wearing it. Having said that…don't make me wear one again. I might just have to kill you."

Rob grinned. "Maybe next time we'll dress up as women. That should fool everyone." He got off the bed. "I guess we'd better hit the sack. It's been a long and eventful day."

Jeff slept quite well, in spite of what he had done. He had committed cold-blooded murder and should feel some kind of guilt, but he didn't. He didn't even feel elated, knowing he had punished the man responsible for Michael's murder. This thing he had been dragged into was far from finished. There were others, more powerful players, involved. They were just as guilty as Anthony Mariano, and they needed to be brought to justice. Michael's murder was only part of something much greater.

After an early breakfast, they drove to the Indianapolis International Airport. Instead of flying to Sacramento, they took a plane to Los Angeles. Rob decided to stay in LA for a few days. "I'd like to visit a friend," he told Jeff.

Jeff flew back to Sacramento. He decided not to go to the hideout in the warehouse. Instead, he went to a motel. The same motel he had used to meet Maxine before he flew to Chicago.

The next day he phoned Barbara from a payphone. "Hi, sis."

"Jeff! I was hoping you might phone sooner. Michael's assets are still frozen. The mortgage company contacted us. They wonder why no payments have been made on Michael's mortgage. They're talking foreclosure. I explained the situation, but those people don't care. They're like a bunch of vultures."

"Have you talked to Mallory, Michael's lawyer?"

"I have. He says his hands are tied."

"He's an idiot. I don't like him. Why Michael ever picked him I'll never know."

"Something else you won't like. Homeland Security confiscated your computer. I had no idea until your Super phoned. He wonders if you're still interested in keeping your apartment. Your lease is coming up for renewal next month. Are you aware of that?"

Jeff sighed. "I am. Don't worry about it. I'll figure something out."

"That man with the accent phoned again. He phones all the time. Why does he want to know where you are? What am I supposed to do, Jeff?"

"I don't know what to tell you. Just ignore him."

"What if he harms the girls?"

"Has he made any threats?"

"Yes, he has. I told you the last time. What if he follows up on his threats?"

"If he phones again, tell him to stop. If he doesn't I'll hunt him down and kill him. Tell him that." His voice sounded harsh and savage.

Barbara was silent for a moment. Then she said, "What happened to you, Jeff? You're scaring me. You've changed. You never ever talked like that."

"I'm sorry. Didn't mean to scare you. Things have happened, Barb. Things I can't explain to you at this time. I can tell you one thing though…I'm making some progress in the investigation of Michael's murder. The guilty ones are being punished."

"How? You're making no sense. We are the only ones being punished right now. Why did this have to happen with Michael? What was he involved in?"

He heard her sob and said, "I promise you this will end soon." He looked at his watch. "I'd better go. How are the girls?"

"They're fine."

"And Angie?"

"She's coping. I'm surprised she's keeping herself together like that. She is a strong girl." She chuckled. "Must be the Chartrand gene."

"Must be. And Omar?"

"He's growing and learning English. He's a smart boy."

"That's good to hear. Take care, Barb. I love you."

"I love you, too. See you soon I hope."

He hung up, a lump in his throat. He'd never asked about Michelle, his daughter, but he knew she was okay. Barbara said the girls were fine. That included Michelle.

The next call he made was to Maxine.

"Jeff," she said. "You're taking a chance contacting me."

"I wanted to hear your voice."

She hesitated. "It would be best if you gave yourself up. I can't help you unless you do."

The way she talked, he realized her phone might be bugged. "I'll give it some thought. I just don't like the five star accommodations I might have to move into. If you don't hear from me within the next seven hours, the answer is probably no."

"Why seven hours?"

"No particular reason." He chuckled. "Let's make it eight hours. It doesn't make any difference to me."

He knew she'd understand what the encrypted message meant.

Meet me at the Five Star Heaven Motel at eight o'clock.

He ate lunch in a small restaurant across the street from the motel. Then he spent the afternoon watching movies in his room. Shortly before eight, he went down into the lobby to wait for Maxine. She showed up at exactly eight. This time, she wore tight pants and a loose sweater. She looked as sexy and delicious as the last time he saw her.

"I always forget how beautiful you are," he said. "You look good enough to eat. I could ravish you right here in the lobby."

She gave him a kiss on the cheek. "Let's not waste any time then," she said, chuckling. "I'm ready for anything you've planned for me tonight."

The moment the door closed behind them, they clung to each other. "Come on," Maxine said huskily. "Don't just stand there. Get undressed and ravish me."

Laughing, they tumbled onto the bed and began undressing each other. He rolled between her opening thighs. For the next half hour, the only sounds in the room were their sighs and moans, and finally her cries of ecstasy and his shout of joy when they reached the apex of their passion. Breathing hard, they lay in each other's arms.

He stroked her naked back and let his hand rest on her buttock. "I love your solid cheeks," he murmured.

"Just my cheeks?" she asked, nibbling his earlobe.

"Your cheeks, you thighs, your hips, your narrow waist, your breasts…"

She laughed softly. "I get the picture. Why don't you just say you love me?"

"I love you."

"Now, was that so hard? I love you too." She kissed him gently. "I'm getting chilly."

"Spend the night with me. I'll keep you warm." He held her in a tight embrace. "I need company tonight."

She didn't hesitate with her answer. "Okay, I'll stay. I've booked off tomorrow. I told Captain Stoneman I want to make this a long weekend."

"Great. I promise I'll make it worth your while."

"You'd better. I want to make love at least two more time before the night is over."

"That's all?"

"Oh, you."

* * * *

"Well, Dr. Callwell from Canada. What fancy restaurant are you going to take me to for breakfast?" Maxine slipped into her tight pants and looked at herself in the mirror.

"Across the street." Jeff chuckled, his eyes on her bare upper body. "Better put on your bra or we'll never get anywhere."

"Promises, that's all I ever get from you," she teased him and thrust out her ample breasts.

Jeff moaned. "Don't tempt me, woman. You're a seductress. I never knew you were such a nymphomaniac."

She laughed. "You never paid any attention to me before. Not as a woman anyway. I was just your partner, that's all."

"I know and I don't know why."

She came up to him and pressed her body against him. Her breasts felt warm and soft on his chest. He put his arms around her and kissed her. Stroking her long blond hair, he looked into her beautiful face, losing himself in the bright blue depth of her eyes. "I was living in the past, Max. After the loss of my wife, I was occupied with feeling sorry for myself. I lost all interest in women. Didn't want to get hurt again, I guess. I don't know."

She smiled. "Well, I'm glad you finally came to your senses." She slipped from his embrace. "Come, let's go and have something to eat. I get moody if I don't have a good breakfast. And you wouldn't want me moody."

The restaurant was quite busy, but they found a booth by the window. Jeff ordered bacon and eggs. Maxine had yogurt and a bagel.

"I thought you wanted to have a hearty breakfast?" Jeff said.

She sighed and eyed his plate. "Believe me, I feel like taking those eggs and that bacon away from you, but how do you think I keep this slim figure?"

"Exercising?" He shrugged.

"That and starving myself." She tasted her coffee and made a face. "They call this coffee? It tastes like wash water."

"Sorry. Next time I'll take you to a better place."

She reached across the table and touched his hand. "Just kidding. It's fine." Her eyes searched his face. "You mumbled something in your sleep last night. I couldn't make it out, but it sounded like *You fat pig*. I hope you didn't dream about me."

He shook his head, smiled. "I wouldn't call you that, not even in my dreams." His face took on a somber expression. "Nicole used to tease me about that. Every time I came back from an assignment I talked in my sleep."

Her eyes never left his face. "Does this mean you've come back from an assignment?"

He sat silent, staring into his plate. Then he looked up and into her eyes. There was no sense in lying to Maxine. She deserved his trust. "What I'm going to tell you must stay with you, Max. Forget that you are a cop. You are off-duty today. This is just between you and me. Okay?"

She nodded.

He spoke with a low voice, making sure nobody was close enough to listen in on their conversation. "Galliano and Mariano had more in common than just their ancestors. Anthony Mariano ordered the hit on Michael. Galliano executed the order. My instincts were right from the beginning."

Maxine didn't speak, but he could tell by her face the information shocked her. "That means Galliano was directly involved in Michael's murder," she said after a while. "This changes a lot. The courts might see this as a good reason to absolve you of Galliano's murder. It was a justified shooting."

"I have to prove my accusations first," he cautioned her.

"How did you find out about this?" she asked.

"I've talked to the Godfather himself." He smiled tightly. "He was probably the one I dreamed about. He's going to haunt my dreams for a long time."

"He told you he gave the order? Did he tell you why?"

"No. That's something I have to find out still. This whole thing is big, Max. I've stumbled into a web of conspiracy and deception, and I won't stop until I find who is behind it all."

Her eyes were grave when she looked at him. "Where you the one who killed Mariano?" When he didn't speak immediately, she lifted a hand. "Maybe you shouldn't answer that, Jeff."

"Are you afraid to hear the truth, Max?"

"Maybe I am afraid where this is leading," she whispered. "I don't know if I can handle it."

He leaned forward. "Michael's murder is only a part of this conspiracy. There are people involved who may be plotting to destroy our country. We have to find out who these people are and stop them. That is why I can't give myself up, Max. I am the only person who has nothing to lose by digging. You don't have to get involved, unless you want to. These people are powerful and ruthless. They have ties to the government and to organized crime." He sat up straight, his face grim. "I'm determined to stop them. Mariano was only the beginning."

"It is all over the news," Maxine said. "I didn't want to mention it last night, but when I saw the videos I knew. I would recognize you anywhere. The way you walk and the way you move. When you knocked out that bodyguard, I was sure. You are a boxer. I've watched you box."

"Do you think others might recognize me?"

She lifted her shoulders. "Probably not. They don't know you the way I do." She smiled. "I kinda liked that ponytail."

"It was not my idea, believe me."

"I didn't think so. You're much to square for that." Her smile lit up her concerned face. "But that's what I like about you. You're not a sheep who follows trends. Maybe sometimes you lag a little behind fashion, but you're a solid citizen with a strong personality and firm principles. A born leader. And a patriot. I believe you when you say you want to punish the people who want to betray our country, but are you sure you're up to it. You are going against people who could squash you and nobody would even cry for you."

"Nobody?" He raised an eyebrow.

"Nobody but me and your immediate family. Most people are just too scared to get involved in what you are planning. Think about it. You've got Galliano and Mariano, the two people who were immediately involved. Are you certain you want to carry on?"

"You forget there are still the men who committed the actual crime. They must be found and punished."

"We will find them. Now that you know about them, we can narrow our search and concentrate on people who were associated with Galliano."

He shook his head. "Knowing what I know, how could I ever sleep again with a clear conscience? You are forgetting about the assassins who killed the other members of my brother's unit. What about your brother Darrin?"

"What about him?"

"Don't you want to know how he died? From what I heard, he was killed by friendly fire. Are you sure he wasn't murdered?"

Her eyes clouded over for a moment and she studied her coffee mug, which she hadn't touched all this time. "Yes, I do want to find out. He's been on my mind lately. Did I tell you I dreamed about him not long ago? I sat in a coffee shop and he walked up to my table and sat down across from me. I said *you are dead.* He smiled and said *no, I'm not dead. Don't let them bury me without saying goodbye.*"

She stared at him, her eyes bright and shiny. "What did he want to tell me, Jeff? I woke up and that dream was so vivid in my memory, I bawled my eyes out. I kept hearing the words he said all day long."

"Maybe he wanted to tell you to find out what happened to him. He wants closure. You want closure. Perhaps it's your subconscious talking to you." He shrugged. "I don't know. I'm not a dream expert."

"Neither am I." Her fingers curled around his. "I worry about you, Jeff. You can't do this alone."

"I'm not alone. I have friends who are with me all the way." His face was sober. "I am trusting you with my life, Max. You could arrest me right now and take me in for questioning. By telling you what you've just heard you are an accomplice and I'm putting your future in jeopardy and your life in danger. Are you sure you want to be part of me and my life?"

There was no hesitation in her answer. "Yes, I do, Jeff. I love you and I would never betray your trust." She smiled. "Besides, you need a friend in the police department. I am that friend."

Chapter Three

They changed motels the same day and checked into a nicer place under the name of Mr. and Mrs. Callwell. The motel had a swimming pool, and they spent much of the day by the pool. In the evening, they danced in the bar. After that, they made love most of the night, until they both dropped from exhaustion.

Saturday, they went for a ride into the country and acted like two people on their honeymoon. Jeff tried to convince himself Maxine was the woman he really loved, but his thoughts began to drift to Connie. He couldn't forget the way he felt the last few days he spent time with her.

July the fourth. Independence Day.

He would forever remember that. He thought then Connie was the woman he loved.

He pushed it out of his mind, determined to let nothing come between him and the happiness he experienced at this moment.

Later, they went out for supper and danced a little. Maxine was quite tipsy by the time they went back to their room. "I am so horny," she giggled, taking off her clothes and throwing them on the floor. Naked, she molded her body into his. "I want to make love to you all night."

He laughed and kissed her. "I won't stop you," he said.

"You're still dressed. That is not fair." She giggled into his mouth. "I think I am just a teensy weensy bit drunk." Plucked on his clothing, she said, "Come on, get naked." She stepped back and looked at him from behind veiled lids. "I believe I was drunk the first time we had sex. It was great."

"Yes, it was." He undressed.

She watched him with a wicked smile on her face. When he was nude, she came up to him and put her hand on his chest. "I want to ride you like a cowgirl." She giggled again and pushed him toward the bed. "On your back, cowboy."

He fell backward onto the soft covers. She climbed on top of the bed and straddled his legs. Looking down at his penis, she said, "I believe I need to stroke this big feller into standing at attention. What kind of a soldier is he?"

"I thought I was a cowboy?" Jeff laughed.

She touched his penis and fondled him. "Soldier, cowboy...what's the difference. As long as he is hard and loyal only to me." She bent forward and kissed the head of his stiffening penis. "Only to me," she whispered.

A stab of guilt began to raise its head and Connie's face hung like a pale ghost in his mind but he was too aroused to let it become more than an annoying thought. At this moment he loved only Maxine. He put his hands on her hips and pulled her toward his stiff mast. "Climb on," he said hoarsely.

She laughed and lifted up, hovering above his aching member. He admired the plump mound of her shaved pussy. It looked so clean and appetizing and he felt like licking it. With agonizing slowness she descended and, touching the tip of his penis with her labia, she rubbed her slit back and forth. Her eyes were closed and from her lips escaped a low moan.

He wanted to push up and shove his organ deep into her but he suppressed the urge, watching her breasts jiggle softly as she moved her body above him. She cried out and jerked her pelvis back and forth; he felt warm liquid running down his penis to soak his pubic hair. Slowly, she sank into his lap, enveloping him with her warm, creamy sheath, moaning loudly as she did so.

Her eyes opened and she whispered, "I love you." Rotating her lower body, she brought herself to a number of orgasms before she stretched out on top of him. "Let's change positions," she sighed. "My legs are getting weak."

He turned with her and moved forcefully between her cradling thighs for a long time.

"I love you so much," she whispered into his ear after they finished making love. "I never knew I could love anyone like this. I want this to never end."

After that they slept through the night. Both of them had come to the end of their endurance.

In the morning, after taking a shower, and feeling refreshed from their sleep, they made love again. They both knew it might be the last time for a while.

Maxine drove away from the motel in the late afternoon. Jeff decided to stay another night, and then he would drive back to the hideout. He wondered about Rob and made up his mind to contact Elias Morgan in hopes of finding out if he had heard from Rob.

That evening, he watched TV for the first time since the day he shot Mariano. Another day he would forever carry with him. Tuesday, July 17, 2007.

He didn't pay too much attention to the news reports until he saw a familiar face.

Ronald Larkin.

"Senator Larkin, now that you've filled the place your father vacated by his untimely death, tell us more about your plans running for the upcoming presidential election. Don't you think it is a bit too soon to be trying for the post of top politician in this country? Shouldn't you get your feet wet first as a Senator? Learn the ropes, so to speak."

Larkin gave the camera his big smile. "I don't think that is necessary. I've been exposed to politics ever since I was a young man. My father has been a politician all of his adult life, and my grandfather before him."

"What qualifies you for the position of President of the United States of America, Senator Larkin?"

"Well, I am thirty-five years old. Born and raised in the United States. I served my country in Iraq." He smiled. "And I'm a lawyer. Many former presidents were lawyers."

The interviewer chuckled. "Yes, that is true. There are rumors that Senator Osborne might be your running mate. That is quite an endorsement."

"Rumors, so far," Larkin said, but he smiled knowingly. "Senator Osborne has been a friend of the family for a long time. He would make a good running mate."

"And President, in case of your demise while in office." The interviewer smiled.

Larkin nodded. "Yes, that is correct. But let's not put the cart before the horse. Much needs to be done before that is even a possibility."

"I hear you have powerful backers for your campaign. There is word that the United Oil Conglomerate is one of them."

"You heard correctly. Herman Weisberg, the CEO, is a good friend. It is only natural that he would help me out."

"I guess it doesn't hurt to be an oilman yourself, doesn't it, Senator Larkin?"

Larkin scowled. "I'm only part owner of Larkin Refineries. Just a silent partner, really. My brother is the CEO and owns the majority of shares. I will pour all of my energy into my job as Senator and," he smiled, "later into the greater job of serving my country."

"I didn't mean to imply anything, Senator. Thank you for taking time out of your busy schedule and chat with us."

"No problem. I'm always available to let the people of America know what I'm up to. There will be no secrets in my camp." Larkin smiled again into the camera and saluted. "Honesty and truth will be the foundation of our time in office."

Jeff pushed the off-button on the remote.

"What fucking bullshit!" he cursed.

Senator Larkin!

I guess he was appointed to the Senate to fill the seat his father vacated. That must have happened while I was in Iraq. Funny, how you're not aware of things when you don't pay attention.

He spent the night in the motel. He checked out early in the morning and drove back to the suite in the warehouse. The place looked undisturbed. If anyone was watching it, there was no indication of that.

He decided to work out in the gym and changed into his trunks. It would do him good to work off his anxiety.

Giving the punching bag a good kick, he watched it swinging back and forth. He turned when he heard the opening of the door and saw someone coming into the gym. It was Rob. "I've managed to crack the code on your brother's flash drive," Rob said as he came closer.

Jeff stopped attacking the punching bag. "That's good news. Did you find anything useful?"

Rob smiled smugly. "That and much more. Not all the news is good, though. It confirms that your brother was involved in the illegal selling of arms. Sorry to be the bearer of bad news."

"Shit!" Jeff smashed his fist into the bag, trying to get rid of his anger and disappointment. *Michael, oh Michael. I thought I knew you.* "What exactly did you find?"

"Records of all the e-mails he received and sent. Orders for weapons."

"Damn it! Who ordered the weapons?"

"The orders originated in Washington. The man who sent them, his name is Tahir Uday. I checked him out. He works for the Iraqi Embassy."

"I can't say that is surprising news," Jeff said. "Where did Michael send those orders?"

"They went to a Paul Clark in St. Louis, Missouri. Clark is an employee of American Defense Manufacturing."

"They manufacture machine guns, assault rifles, and ammunition. They also build tanks, helicopters and planes," Jeff mused. "I assume you did more digging."

"I did. Guess who owns a large portion of shares in that company?"

Jeff shook his head, conveying his ignorance. "Who?"

"Our dear Colonel James O'Connor owns fifteen percent, and his brother Harry a whopping twenty percent. That means they own thirty-five percent between them. It's almost like a family owned business."

"That still doesn't mean they're involved in illegal arms trading. We can't let our feelings for the Colonel influence us, even though it is tempting."

"No, but I bet your ass they are mixed up in it. You can't run a business and not know what is going on. We're not so naïve not to come to those conclusions. Why else would O'Connor be so interested in getting rid of my father and closing down Grey Ops? He doesn't want anyone digging around. That's why."

Jeff pondered Rob's deductions and had to admit, the evidence was overwhelming. If Colonel O'Connor were involved, then he would do anything to stop anyone from finding out. Including murder. But did he have anything to do with Michael's murder? The orders came from Mariano.

"What about Mariano's files?" he asked.

Rob shrugged. "Nothing yet. He used an advanced encryption program. But don't worry, we'll crack it eventually. My friend Freddy Golden is a computer nerd. If anyone can do it, he's the one."

Jeff smiled. "I thought *you* were the computer whiz kid?"

"I am, but I'm not as good as Freddy." He chuckled. "He's not the most handsome guy. Women scare the hell out of him. Mind you, that doesn't mean he's gay, just shy, but he has a way with computers. I wish I had his talent." He grinned. "Of course, I'd rather be successful with women. That's more fun."

Jeff smiled, remembering Rob's escapades in Dallas and in Chicago. "More fun you may have with women, but I'd say they are also your weakness."

Rob sighed. "You might just be right, o' Wise One." He became serious again. "Oh, I forgot to mention Mariano also was one of the major shareholders of American Defense Manufacturing."

"That means the O'Connor brothers and Mariano knew each other," Jeff said. "Could they have been responsible for my brother's murder? It makes no sense. After all, he was the one communicating with the insurgents. In a way he worked for the O'Connor brothers." Jeff felt sudden anger rising in him again. "If they're guilty, I'll kill those bastards with my bare hands," he said between clenched teeth.

"We have no proof," Rob cautioned. "Like you said, what reason would they have for killing him?"

"I don't know, but what reason did Mariano have for ordering a hit on my brother? Mariano was a businessman and a mobster. He was a racketeer, involved in money laundering, drugs, and prostitution. Possibly even in the trading of young girls and boys, and in pornography. You name it. Anything that creates money. I'm sure murder was also part of his agenda. But what did Michael do to Mariano to invite being put on his hit list?"

"Mariano may not have had a reason. Perhaps he did someone a favor." Rob lifted his shoulders and spread his hands in a gesture that meant he had no idea.

"Did you get anything from the files you downloaded from Hardini?" Jeff asked.

Rob nodded. "Enough. According to the records, Mariano was the sole owner of Nova Investments. Hardini worked for him. It also contained copies of e-mails sent to and received from someone at American Defense Manufacturing. If you guessed Paul Clark, you guessed right. And he kept copies of the e-mails he had our unfortunate friend Jimmy Marco send to Moore's Exotic Exports. He must have had a reason for keeping those copies. Everything was quite detailed."

"Too bad we can't talk to him. He might spill the beans now that his boss Mariano is dead."

"Want to go for lunch?" Rob asked.

"Sure, but I'd like to workout for a while. Been neglecting it. I think I'm gaining weight." He pinched his midriff." My belly muscles are getting soft and mushy."

Rob chuckled, looking at Jeff's washboard belly. "I hope I'll be in the shape you're in when I reach your ripe age. How about going a round, *old man*?"

"Are you sure you want to fight an old guy like me?" Jeff asked, smiling.

"I promise I'll be gentle," Rob said, laughing. "Just let me change into my trunks."

* * * *

The waitress gave Jeff a little smile when she took his order.

"Hi, Julia," he said, returning her smile.

"I was hoping you'd call," she said in a low voice.

"I would have, but something else came up." Jeff felt a twinge of guilt when he looked into her dark almond eyes. She looked so vibrant, so young. And full of promise. To stare into those beautiful eyes in the throes of passion would have been a wonderful experience.

That was the problem though. She was too damned young. He could be her father.

"Too bad," she said.

He thought he could detect regret in her voice and smile and felt momentary sadness for a missed opportunity. "It's never too late," he heard himself say.

She was still smiling. "Sometimes it is," she said. "I have a new boyfriend."

"I'm glad to hear that," he said, not glad at all, but he managed to smile. "I'm jealous. He's a lucky guy. I guess I've missed my chance."

She laughed. "For now anyway, but you never know what happens." She looked at Rob. "What can I get you?"

Rob had been listening to the conversation between her and Jeff with amused interest. "I'll have the special," he said.

She nodded. "Okay."

He watched her as she walked away. Then, with a grin, he looked at Jeff. "Did I miss something here?"

Jeff smiled. "Nothing of great interest to you, my young nosy friend."

"Wow," Rob said. "I'll have to give it to you. You still have it in you."

"Oh, shut up!" Jeff chuckled. He felt almost embarrassed, like a man whose great secret has suddenly been exposed. "She's just an elusive dream. A piece of candy I wouldn't mind having but forbidden to touch. Happy?"

Rob nodded. His lips smiled, but his eyes were serious. "I understand. Must be tough. I don't know if I could be that strong."

"You will, you will." Jeff sighed. "There is something else I'd like

30

to discuss with you. My sister has been getting threatening phone calls by someone with an accent. I'm wondering if there is any way you could find out where these calls originate."

"I could. I would have to install a tracer in your sister's phone."

"Can you do it?"

"Sure. When?"

"How about tomorrow morning? If I give you her number, would you phone her and make an appointment for tomorrow. Tell her you're from the phone company, just in case her phone is bugged."

"No problem." Rob looked up when Julia came with a pitcher of water and let her fill his glass. "Has my father here been hitting on you?" he asked her, grinning.

"Your father?" She stared at him and then at Jeff.

Jeff shook his head. "He's pulling your leg. I'm no more his father than I'm yours." He chuckled. "I'm too young for that. This beard makes me look older."

She tilted her head. "So shave it off."

"You may not like me anymore when you see me without it. It's supposed to make me look sophisticated."

This beard is a fake anyway. And so is the red color of my hair.

She touched his shoulder, as if by accident. "I doubt shaving off your beard will make you less handsome." Her laughter teased him. "Your food will be ready in a minute."

He looked after her and sighed.

Rob didn't comment, just shook his head. "Give me your sister's number. I'll call her right now, if you want."

Jeff scribbled Barbara's number on a piece of paper and handed it to Rob.

Rob pulled out his cell phone and dialed the number. "This is the phone company," he said, "would it be all right if we send someone over tomorrow morning to check out your phone, Mrs. Helmann?"

He paused for a moment. "No, there is no problem. This is just a routine maintenance check." He paused again. "All right, we'll see you at ten."

He put away his phone. "You heard. It's arranged. By the way, your sister has a nice voice."

"She's married, you moron. And much too old for you. Let me warn you, my horny young friend…you make a play for her and you will have to deal with her husband. He's German and Reinhart's buddy from

31

School. Need I tell you more?"

Rob snickered. "I'm shaking with fear, Mother-hen."

* * * *

In the evening, Jeff watched TV, trying to catch up with events in the world. As usual, he only watched with passing interest, reading a book during commercials. He almost missed it, when the announcer said, "We have a special report from our sister station in Fresno."

The face of a reporter who looked familiar appeared on the screen. "Tonight, we bring you a follow-up on an interview we had with a Miss Connie Wu a couple of weeks ago concerning the murder of her friend Mr. Dennis Wu, a decorated war hero."

Connie's face filled the screen briefly, then the camera moved back to show Connie and the interviewer.

"Welcome again to our show, Miss Wu. You have indicated that you have uncovered more information on the murder of Mr. Kim. Can you tell us more about that?"

"Certainly. After going through the possessions of my late friend Dennis, I found evidence that his murder has something to do with his mission in Iraq. You see he belonged to a special unit. The unit's CO was Ronald Larkin."

"Do you mean Senator Larkin?"

"Yes. Senator Larkin. The same man who is rumored to be running for President. He had the rank of lieutenant when Dennis served with him. There were ten men altogether in that unit. They called themselves the *Ten Commandos.* "

"Why?"

Connie shrugged. "I don't know. You'd have to ask the members of that group." She gave a crooked smile. "Unfortunately, most of them are dead."

"I don't quite understand. Were they killed in combat?" The interviewer leaned forward, waiting for Connie to answer.

"No. They were murdered."

"Murdered? That has an ominous sound to it." He looked into the camera as it zoomed in on him. "We'll come back to Miss Wu after the commercial break."

What the fuck! Jeff cursed silently.

What are you doing, Connie? Don't mention my name, whatever you're going to say.

With disgust, he watched a commercial that showed paratroopers jumping out of a plane. And another showing marines storming some kind of building, guns blazing. Then a soldier carrying a wounded child out of the building.

Uncle Sam wants you!

Shit! When are they ever going to stop glorifying the army and war!

"We are back with Miss Wu." The reporter looked expectantly at Connie. "You told us that the men in Mr. Kim's unit did not die in combat but that they were murdered? Do you have proof of that?"

Connie chuckled, her expression anything but pleasant. She held up a picture. "These are the ten soldiers of that unit."

She waited until the camera zoomed in on the picture. "From left to right. Captain Ronald Larkin. Staff-sergeant John Parker. John MacKay, killed in Iraq by so-called friendly fire. James Carrington, Brian McGee, both men still alive, I believe. All of the men on McGee's right are dead. Toby Miller, who died two weeks before the attempt on Dennis. Murdered in an apparent robbery. Together with his wife. Ethan Grey, killed in a shootout. Dennis Kim. Murdered May 7th. Shot to death. Michael Chartrand. Murdered March 19. Shot to death. With him died his wife and his fourteen-year-old son. And the last man in the picture is Darrin Montana, killed in Iraq by friendly fire."

Connie's words were full of irony. "So it says in the report."

"You don't believe that?"

"What does it really matter what I believe? I just find it a coincidence that so many men who served together defending their country meet such violent deaths after they come back home. What happened over there that warrants their execution?"

She looked straight into the camera. "What did these men know that made them so dangerous they had to be silenced? Who are the people behind these murders?"

"Are implying there is some kind of conspiracy, or possibly some cover-up, Miss Wu?" the reporter said, his voice dramatic, his expression somber.

"Call it what you will. Mark my words it isn't over yet. There were ten men in that unit. Six are dead. Four are still alive. For how long?"

The report stopped abruptly and the next face on the screen was that of the local news reporter. "Wow!" she said to another reporter sitting at the desk beside her. "That sounds almost like something from a mystery novel. Do you think Senator Larkin's life is in danger?"

The other reporter shrugged. "One might almost think that. I hope the Senator has loyal bodyguards. If I were in his shoes, I would certainly look into this woman's allegations. Fortunately, he is in a position to do so."

The camera focused on his face. "And now to sports…"

Chapter Four

Rob picked up Jeff shortly after eight. Enough time to go for breakfast and then drive to Barbara's home.

Jeff didn't want to worry Barbara, and he decided to accompany Rob. If the house should be watched, which he doubted but still considered a possibility, the watchers would not be alarmed to see a delivery van parking in front of her house.

Rob carried a tools box, while Jeff held a small attaché case under his arm.

He had to give Barbara credit for the way she reacted when she saw him standing on her doorsteps.

"You must be the telephone people," she said, stepping back to let them in.

After the door closed behind Jeff, Barbara was in his arms. "It is so good to see you," she said, holding him in a tight embrace. Then she looked into his face with tearstained eyes and smiled. "You've still got that red beard."

He chuckled. "I'm beginning to like it."

She let go of him and looked questioningly at Rob. "You're not from the telephone company, are you?"

Rob grinned. "No, Ma'am. I'm not."

"This is Rob. A friend of mine," Jeff said. "He's going to install a tracer in your phone line. We'll find out who that man with the accent is."

"You can do that?" Barbara walked toward the kitchen. "Want a cup of coffee? I just finished brewing a pot."

"Sure," Rob said. He followed Jeff into the kitchen and looked around. "Nice place you have here, Mrs. Helmann?"

"Thank you. Please, call me Barb. All my friends do." She got a couple of mugs from the cupboard and filled them. Putting the mugs on the table, she looked at Jeff. "How are you doing, Jeff? It's been nearly three weeks since I saw you last. I wanted so much to give you a hug

35

then. I hate this cloak and dagger stuff. How can you live with that?"

Jeff shrugged. "You get used to it. You'd be amazed what you can do when your survival is at stake." He took a sip from his mug. "Good coffee, sis."

"If you'd be around more, you could drink it more often." She smiled. "How long is this going to go on, Jeff? Will there ever be an end?"

"I hope so." When he heard the patter of naked feet on the hardwood floor, he looked to the entrance of the living room. Then he stared at the little boy standing under the arch, looking at him with large eyes.

Barbara went and took the boy's hand. "Omar, come and say *hi* to your uncle Jeff."

She turned to Jeff and said, "This is Michael's son Omar."

Jeff smiled. "I know. We've met."

Her eyes questioned.

"Omar didn't just get picked up in Iraq and brought over here. It wasn't easy getting him out. Omar's been through a lot and he is lucky to be alive. He was in the hands of kidnappers who would surely have murdered him."

"I don't understand. What are you telling me?"

"I was the one who rescued him from the kidnappers, Barb." He didn't see any harm in telling her. He had to trust somebody with the events in his life. She was his sister. If he couldn't trust her, who else was there?

"You?" He saw the disbelief. "How?"

"You wanted to know where I was all this time? Not in jail. I was in Iraq, looking for Omar. Now is not the time to go into details. Just be happy Michael's son is with you…with us. There was nobody else I could trust with the job of getting him out alive."

He saw the tears running down her face, as she suddenly understood. "How can you bear all of this, Jeff? I wish I could do more. I feel so helpless."

"You are doing more than enough, Barb. How are the girls?"

She wiped her tears. "They are doing fine. Michelle has been asking for you. She loves you very much, Jeff. She knows you're her father, don't ever forget that."

Jeff swallowed down a sudden lump in his throat. "I love her too. I've never forgotten she's my daughter and I wish things could have turned out differently." He reached out and touched her hand. "I'll

36

always be grateful for the sacrifice you've made."

She smiled and squeezed his hand. "It was never a sacrifice. I love her like my own daughter. And so does Helmut."

Rob, who had been silent, finished his coffee. "I'd better get started," he said, getting up. "Where is your main connection into the house, Barb?"

"In the basement. Just go down the stairs, turn to your right and you'll see a door. The electric panel is in the storage room behind that door."

"I'll find it. It won't take me long."

Rob walked to the stairs. Jeff heard his steps on the wooden steps. "He's a very special young man," he said. "He was with me in Iraq."

"He doesn't look that old," Barbara said.

Jeff had to laugh. "I don't mean then. I'm talking about when we rescued Omar."

"Oh." She giggled and put a hand over her mouth. "I'm glad he didn't hear me. I wouldn't want to hurt his feelings."

"I don't think you can." Jeff smiled, glad to see her regaining her sense of humor. "He's as tough as they come."

And as cold.

Jeff remembered the efficiency he had displayed executing Lieutenant George Stiller. He had followed Jeff's order without question and without showing remorse.

"He reminds me a little of you when you were younger," Barbara said.

How perceptive you are, sis. I see that also. And that's what scares me. When did I lose my compassion for my fellow man? Do I still have feelings left in me? Can I still love the way I used to love? Is the coldness I feel inside me so obvious, dear sister?

He smiled, trying to hide his thoughts. "Have you talked to Maxine lately?"

"No, not for a few days. And you?"

"We've been in touch," he said. Even though he felt guilty about not being honest with Barbara, he nevertheless didn't think it was a good idea for her to know about the weekend he spent with Maxine. He knew she wouldn't tell anyone, but he didn't want to hurt her feelings, didn't want her to assume he cared more about Maxine than his own sister.

"He's already learned a few words," Barbara said. "Come here, Omar, don't be shy."

The little boy was studying Jeff with his large eyes. If he ever had any doubts that this little boy was his brother's son, looking into Omar's blue eyes removed all doubt.

This was Michael's son. His nephew.

Jeff put his hand on the boy's head. "Hi, Omar. I'm your uncle Jeff." He chuckled, suddenly remembering that he was in disguise. "Once I'm back to my old self, you'll have to get to know me all over again."

"Jeff," Omar said, smiling. Then he pointed to himself. "My name is Omar Helmann."

Barbara laughed at Jeff's puzzled expression. "I was just as shocked to find out I had a son," she said. "But when they brought him, that's what his papers said…Omar Helmann."

"I had no hand in that. They promised me everything would be taken care of. I guess it was the only way." Jeff thought of his brother-in-law. "What did Helmut say?"

"Oh, he was tickled pink. He's always wanted a son. Omar's blue eyes didn't hurt either to convince Helmut. Makes him appear German."

Jeff laughed. "Heaven forbid that Omar should take that too literally. We don't want him growing up speaking with a German accent."

Barbara joined his laughter. "There is a good chance of that if Helmut spends too much time with him."

They both had to laugh even louder when Omar let out a little giggle.

Jeff's attention was diverted from the little boy when he heard Rob coming up the stairs. "All done," Rob said. "Now we hope that man phones again soon."

"Don't worry, he will. He won't leave us alone until somebody stops him," Barbara said.

"We will stop him. That's a promise." Rob looked at Jeff. "We should be going before someone becomes suspicious about the van."

"All right."

He gave Barbara a hug and a kiss on the cheek. She held onto him for a moment. "Be careful, Jeff. I worry about you. You're the only brother I've got left."

"I will. You take care of yourself too."

* * * *

Rob came back to the warehouse the next morning. Jeff was already working out in the gym.

"Well, I've got him," Rob said. "He phoned your sister last night. I traced the call and found that it comes from someone in Washington." He smiled smugly. "The phone number belongs to a man by the name of Tahir Uday. The same man who ordered the weapons from your brother."

"That son of a bitch!" The punching bag swung violently back and forth as Jeff kicked it vehemently. "These people come to our country, hide behind their immunity status and they think they can get away with this shit. I'll show him differently."

"What do you have in mind?"

"I'm going to fly to Washington and confront the man. Maybe lean on him a little. Let him know that we're on to him and there will be no more arms shipments."

Rob smiled. "Funny, I had the same idea. When do you want to leave?"

"There is no better time than now. How about tomorrow? Unless you have something else planned."

"Nothing. I'm still on leave."

They worked out silently for a while, first alone and then they sparred on the mat for thirty minutes. Rob surprised Jeff again with his agility and strength. Jeff had to work hard to keep up with the younger man.

"You are the best," Rob complimented Jeff. "It's a pleasure to practice with someone of your caliber. Most of the guys I know can't touch you when it comes to finesse and endurance. I'm actually surprised."

Jeff avoided one of Rob's vicious kicks and went into the offensive. "Are you saying that because of my age?"

"To be truthful, yes. Your age and your size." Rob dropped and moved back, barely evading Jeff's punch. He held up both of his hands. "I'm giving up, big man. One kick in the balls is enough for one day."

Jeff laughed and let his arms drop, but still staying vigilant. With Rob, one had to be on guard at all times. He had a way of tricking you into believing you were safe, but not this time. Rob held out his hand. "Thanks for your friendship, Jeff. I value it. You are one of the few people I would trust with my life."

"Well, thanks, buddy." Jeff shook the offered hand. "I feel the same way about you. You are a remarkable young man. Your father should be proud of you. Speaking of your father, have you heard from him?"

Rob shook his head. "He has dropped out of sight. I don't know where he is."

"Are you worried about his safety?"

"A little, but he's a crafty old man and knows how to take care of himself. I never told you, he is not well. He thinks I don't know about it, but his heart is giving him trouble. Problem is he is just so damn stubborn. Won't quit his job because there is nobody who could take over from him. Anyway, that's what he thinks."

"Maybe he's right. Who would there be?"

Rob gave Jeff a long look. "There is one person my father always spoke highly of. His name came up many times in conversations."

"Do I know the guy?"

"You do," Rob said solemnly. "It's you."

"Me?" Jeff shook his head. "Come on, Rob. I left Grey Ops sixteen years ago. So much has changed. I lost touch. Why would you or your father even think of me?"

"I told you when we first met that you are a bit of a legend in the Corporation. Quite a bit. Your conduct in Iraq established why. You are the logical heir of Colonel Cowley's position. All you have to do is join the ranks of the Military again, I mean officially, and my father would see to it that your name comes up. He has a lot of clout in Washington."

"Can he make me a Colonel?"

"He can recommend it."

Jeff did a few stretches and went through a couple of moves. "Let's hit the showers."

While standing under the shower, he pondered Rob's suggestions. Would he really be interested in taking over Colonel Cowley's job? He wasn't sure about that. Rob's plan had one flaw. He didn't take into account Colonel O'Connor.

Cowley had been suspended from his job. O'Connor would not let another man, one who was in reality still a civilian, just come in and slide into a position he might desire himself. Besides, O'Connor wanted to dissolve Grey Ops, not have it re-established under a different leader.

Jeff shut off the spray of water and stepped out of the shower, looking for a towel. Rob was already dressing himself and waited for him until he was ready to leave the locker room.

They had almost reached the door to the gym, when it burst open and a number of men in army fatigues burst into the room. Jeff registered automatically that they were Military Police. The M-16s in their hands left no doubt that they hadn't dropped in for a friendly chat.

He instinctively fell into a fighting stance. From the corner of his eyes, he saw Rob do the same.

"Don't try to resist or we'll open fire!" shouted one of the intruders.

Jeff knew that resistance would have been pointless. He straightened out and lifted his hands into the air.

The men, Jeff counted eight of them, spread out in the gym and did a search.

"Anyone else in the building?"

Jeff looked at the speaker. "Who the fuck are you and what is this all about?"

"I am Lieutenant Wishnowski. Are you Jeff Chartrand?"

"What if I am?"

"Then you're under arrest!" He looked at Rob. "And so are you, Specialist Masters."

"By whose orders?" Rob challenged him.

"Colonel O'Connor gave the order."

"What are the charges?"

"Murder." Wishnowski waved his weapon. "We have orders to shoot and kill if necessary. Make it easy and give yourself up, let us cuff you without fuss and spare us the tasteless job of killing a fellow soldier."

Rob chuckled. "You'd die before me," he said.

"Don't even think about it," Wishnowski said sharply.

Jeff detected a note of near panic in the man's voice and wondered what O'Connor had told them about Rob and him. The lieutenant was young. He'd probably never seen action on the battlefield.

"You ever kill a man?" Jeff asked the young lieutenant.

"Does it matter?"

"The first one is the hardest. He will haunt your dreams for a long time. Killing another human from close is not the same as shooting at one from far away. An enemy who is close enough to touch is also the most dangerous. Being careless could cost you your life. And you are careless, Lieutenant."

He took a step forward. The other man's machine gun came up, but much too slow.

"Had I wanted to kill you, you'd be dead now," Jeff said with a low voice. "I've been in tighter situations than this one and walked away the winner. I'm letting you live because your death would serve no purpose."

Wishnowski broke into sudden laughter. "A wonderful show of bravado. Eight armed trained soldiers against two unarmed men? Come on, don't be stupid."

"I'm just trying to give you some advice for the next time. You have seven men with you. All of them doing nothing but searching aimlessly for an enemy who may or may not be hiding somewhere, when all you need are two men to do that job. The other five should be guarding us. We are the immediate danger." Jeff chuckled. "And you, Lieutenant Wishnowski, you are standing much too close to me."

The lieutenant involuntarily took a step backward.

Jeff watched the other soldiers milling around. The knuckles of the one nearest to him were white as he held his weapon in a tight grip.

"Relax, soldier," Jeff said to him. "We have no intentions of fighting you." He nodded to Rob. "Right?"

Rob gave him a grim smile. "Whatever you say, Lieutenant."

Wishnowski threw a surprised glance at Jeff. "Lieutenant?" he asked.

Jeff nodded. "I saw action when you were still trying to figure out how you could get laid while in high school." He chuckled when Wishnowski pulled his brows together. "Just for your information, I was in Kuwait during the Gulf War. Many good men died in that war, some of them my best friends. I received a medal of bravery for defending this country, so the next time you and I meet, I expect you show more respect for a fellow officer."

"I wasn't told you were a lieutenant," Wishnowski defended his actions.

"I accept that," Jeff said. "There is no need to put us into chains. We'll come freely. This is all a big mistake anyway." He glanced at Rob. "Let's follow these fine soldiers peacefully."

Jeff didn't feel as confident as he sounded. Murder? Whose murder?

Why would O'Connor send a squad of armed soldiers to arrest him and Rob? Certainly not for the execution of Mariano! Should he somehow be implicated of that, he'd be facing a couple of FBI agents and a SWAT team now instead of a number of MPs.

He shrugged. He'd find out soon enough.

"How did you locate us here?" he asked the lieutenant.

Wishnowski shook his head. "We were given an order, that's all I know. Now, please, follow us. I appreciate your co-operation,

Lieutenant."

They were taken to a closed army van and put inside. Six of the soldiers joined Jeff and Rob in the box. Jeff smiled when he saw the tension in the men's posture, in the way they held their weapons.

What were they told about us? Are we such dangerous criminals?

"Been an MP for long?" he asked one of the men, the same one he had already addressed before. He looked young, like someone fresh from training camp.

The young man hesitated. He threw a glance at his teammates before he answered. "A couple of months."

"I'm Lieutenant Chartrand, soldier." Jeff spoke softly but the meaning of his words was clear.

"Yes, sir."

"It never hurts to be polite and civil, even to someone in shackles, soldier. Maybe someday you'll be under my command. What's your name?"

"Marc St Germaine, sir." The soldier shifted uneasily on his seat, held on to his machine gun with frozen fingers.

"Relax, St Germaine. You're the man with the weapon. We are unarmed." Jeff chuckled. "But that doesn't mean you should drop your guard. Let me give you some friendly advice. Never engage in a conversation with a prisoner. Never take your eyes off a prisoner, no matter how harmless he may appear. Your life may depend on that. Understood."

"Yes, sir, Lieutenant."

Rob laughed beside Jeff. "You guys have a lot to learn. I, for one, would have never left two criminals like us unchained." He lowered his voice, but it rang clear in the confines of the van. "Your lieutenant is a fool to put you in the same box with us. If you think that just because you have the guns means that you are safe, you are wrong. Having guns puts you in even more danger than you can imagine."

His laughter sounded hollow when all eyes stared at him.

"Shut up!" one of the men said. His eyes flickered to Jeff.

Rob grinned. "They obviously have no idea who we are," he said to Jeff.

"I told you to shut up."

Rob glared at the speaker. "If we were a couple of terrorists, you'd be dead already. We could easily disarm you, kill you, and shoot our way out of this vehicle."

"Just try it, buddy." The soldier moved his machine gun in a threatening gesture.

"Take it easy," Jeff said soothingly. "My friend is only trying to mess with your mind. He is right, though. Don't put all your faith in your weapons. They can easily be used against you. Use your brain and stay vigilant at all times."

The vehicle stopped after an hour. When the doors opened, Jeff noticed they were on the army base he had been on before. The soldiers marched them into one of the buildings and put them into a prison cell.

Jeff took a seat on the bench and stared at Rob. "How did they know where to find us?" he asked.

Rob shrugged his shoulders and shook his head. "I guess in a way it's my fault. I should have been more heedful and swept the place every time I came to visit. Either someone talked out of school or they had the place watched."

Jeff sighed. "I guess it doesn't matter. Why do you think O'Connor had us arrested?"

Rob put a finger to his mouth, as if giving Jeff's question some thought, but Jeff read the gesture correctly. "I haven't the faintest idea," Rob said.

Jeff looked around in the cell, spotted the camera that looked like a smoke detector on the ceiling. "I hope they don't let us wait too long before we're told," he said. "I haven't even had breakfast yet."

Rob joined Jeff on the bench. "O'Connor will be fishing." His voice was barely a whisper and Jeff had to strain to hear him. "He has nothing, remember that."

Jeff sighed. "I hope you're right."

Chapter Five

Jeff glanced at Rob, who sat beside him. Then he looked at the presiding investigating officer. No surprise there. He expected to see him.

Colonel O'Connor.

This was not a court-martial, just an investigation known as the Article 32 hearing, but he knew O'Connor would try his best to move it to a higher court as quickly as possible.

The gaunt face of Colonel O'Connor turned to look at Jeff. One look into the Colonel's blue cold eyes convinced Jeff he meant to bury him.

Jeff didn't know the man beside the Colonel. He wore civilian clothes, but that didn't mean that he was not a military man. Jeff wondered who he was. Somehow, he looked familiar.

The eyes of O'Connor still rested on Jeff. "Lieutenant Chartrand, would you please rise."

Jeff rose and looked expectantly at the Colonel.

"Lieutenant Jeffrey Chartrand, this is an investigation into the death of one Lieutenant George Stiller." He paused to let it sink in. Then he carried on. "You have been charged with the murder of Lieutenant George Stiller in Iraq the night of June twenty-two, 2007. How do you plead?"

"I plead not guilty. I have never heard of that man."

O'Connor's eyes bored into his. "May I remind you that you are under oath, Lieutenant?"

"No need to remind me, sir. It will not change anything I'm saying."

The Colonel's eyes shifted to Rob. "Specialist Robert Masters. Please rise."

He waited until Rob had followed his request. "Specialist Masters, you are also charged with the murder of Lieutenant George Stiller. How do you plead?"

"Not guilty, sir." Rob's voice sounded cool and calm.

The Colonel turned to the man sitting beside him. "This is Mr.

45

Gerald Stiller. He is the father of Lieutenant George Stiller. We have asked him to sit in on the hearing. Since he is a lawyer, we have allowed him to cross-examine you."

Stiller rose. Looking into his face, Jeff saw the resemblance to his son. The same swarthy face, the same cruel mouth. "I will see to it that you face a firing squad, you son of a bitch!" the man shouted.

"No obscene language, please, and no threats," O'Connor advised him.

"This man murdered my son." Stiller almost sobbed. "He had him executed in cold blood. He didn't even have the decency to have his body shipped back home to let us give him a proper burial. No, he buried him in the sand like an animal. I want that man punished!"

"If he is guilty he will be punished," O'Connor said. "Begin your cross-examination."

Stiller stepped onto the floor and came closer. "Give me one reason why you did this?"

Jeff looked him straight in the eyes. "I'm sorry. I have absolutely no idea what this is all about. I've never met your son. Where was he murdered?"

"In Iraq, as if you didn't know."

"What was he doing in Iraq?"

"He was there on a secret mission." Stiller stared at him. "I'm asking the questions, not you."

"You are wrong, sir. This is a hearing, not a court. I am allowed to examine the evidence and to cross-examine witnesses, just like you." Jeff spoke calmly. "Who is my accuser? I don't see anyone here who saw this alleged murder take place."

Stiller looked back at O'Connor. The Colonel waved him back. "Please return to your seat, Mr. Stiller. We will produce a witness."

Jeff heard the faint sound of a door opening. He turned to see who was coming through the door. He had a good memory for faces. The soldier who walked in looked familiar, but Jeff couldn't place him at the moment.

The soldier approached the desk and waited for orders. "Please state you name and rank," O'Connor said.

"Raymond Gurney. Private. Sir."

"Private Gurney, can you tell us where you were June twenty-two, 2007."

"In Iraq, sir."

"What did you do in Iraq?"

"Defending my country, sir?"

"What exactly did you do on the date in question?"

"I was taking part in a secret mission, sir."

"And what was this secret mission, Private?"

"We were delivering a shipment of arms to a group of Iraqi freedom fighters."

"Let me repeat that, Private. You were delivering arms to a group of Iraqi freedom fighters. Is that correct?"

"That is correct, sir."

Son of a bitch. Where the hell was this going? Jeff didn't dare glance at Rob.

"May I ask you why you would secretly deliver arms to such a group?"

"I can't tell you, sir. I just followed orders."

"Was Lieutenant George Stiller one of the men accompanying that shipment of arms?"

"Yes, he was the one in charge."

"What happened that night, after you arrived at the camp where you were supposed to deliver the weapons?"

"I don't know exactly what went down, sir. I was hiding in a covered truck. After our truck stopped, we heard gunfire. Then we were told to climb off the truck by a group of American soldiers who, apparently, killed all of the Iraqi fighters we were supposed to deliver the weapons to. The commander of the group gave the order to execute the Lieutenant."

"Do you see that man in this room?"

Gurney looked around the room. Then he shook his head. "No, I don't, sir."

"What?" Gerald Stiller shouted. "He's right over there!"

O'Connor threw Stiller a reprimanding look. "Please, calm yourself, sir." He looked at Gurney. "Are you sure, Private?"

"I'm sure."

"What about the man who shot Lieutenant Stiller? Do you see him?"

"Again, the young soldier looked around. His eyes fell on Rob. He pointed. "He could be the man, but I'm not sure. It was dark and everything happened so quickly."

"You see a man who might be the one who shot your lieutenant, but you don't see the man who gave the order?" O'Connor asked. "Is that correct?"

"That is correct, sir."

Jeff suddenly understood. Of course the soldiers would not be able to identify him with his red hair and beard. He was safe as long as he kept his mouth shut. And he had no intentions to open it, unless absolutely necessary. The reason Gurney couldn't identify Rob was simple enough. Rob had shaved off his mustache.

O'Connor gave Jeff a long look, and then he turned his attention back to Gurney. "The man who gave the order to execute Lieutenant Stiller, what was his name?"

"I heard him introduce himself as Lieutenant Rant, or something like that. I don't remember exactly. I was afraid for my life."

"Did it sound like Chartrand?"

"Maybe. Like I said, I was afraid I might get shot."

"Anything else you remember?"

"No, sir."

O'Connor didn't look happy. "You are dismissed, Private Gurney."

When Gurney walked past Jeff and Rob, he threw a quick glance at Rob but ignored Jeff.

Glaring at Rob, O'Connor said, "Considering the testimony of Private Gurney, are you willing to change your plea, Specialist Masters?"

"No, I am not. I stand by what I said, sir. He really didn't identify me, sir."

"Would you be willing to testify against Lieutenant Chartrand if I guarantee you immunity?"

"No, sir. I have no reason to do that, since I'm innocent of the charge."

O'Connor threw up his hands. "You are making a mistake. It is only a matter of time before I will produce evidence that finds you and Lieutenant Chartrand guilty of this offense. We will proceed tomorrow."

"I request the presence of a councilor," Rob said.

"Council will be provided."

"No, I want my own. I request Elias Morgan of Cohen, Markus and Drexler to represent us."

"This is only a hearing. No need to bring in a civilian lawyer. He may not be familiar with the proceedings of a military court."

"As you said, this is only a hearing. Elias Morgan is no civilian. He is a retired Captain and quite familiar with the courts of the Military."

O'Connor sighed. "Very well. How about you, Lieutenant Chartrand?"

"I am quite satisfied having Captain Morgan represent me, sir."

Jeff could hear Stiller talking loudly to the Colonel. It was obvious, he was not happy with the way things had developed. He breathed a sigh of relief when he was back in his cell.

He was alone. They had decided to put Rob into another cell.

Jeff stretched out on the narrow bed and closed his eyes. He knew O'Connor was out for blood and would not rest until he dug up enough to bury him and Rob. And possibly the rest of Grey Ops.

He wondered what had happened to Colonel Cowley.

* * * *

It seemed he hadn't slept at all. Sitting on the bench in front of O'Connor, he had a feeling of déjà vu.

He looked at the corpulent man standing on the floor…Captain Elias Morgan and he hoped the man was as good a lawyer as Rob assured him.

The young soldier sitting in the witness stand looked expectantly at Morgan.

"I wasn't here yesterday and therefore I need to ask you some questions you may have been asked before. Your name is Raymond Gurney. Private Raymond Gurney. Is that correct?"

"That is correct, sir."

Morgan smiled. "I'm not in the Military anymore, young man. Let's dispense with formalities." He paused. "I have a transcript here of yesterday's proceedings. I'm not going to repeat every question you were asked. You said you were in Iraq on June twenty-two, 2007. Correct?"

"That is correct, sir."

"Just relax, young man. You don't have to call me sir. All right?"

Gurney nodded. "All right."

"You took part in a secret mission to deliver arms to a subversive group?"

"Not subversive. Freedom fighters."

"Okay, freedom fighters." Morgan chuckled. "They all call themselves freedom fighters, but that is neither here nor there. Instead of freedom fighters, you encountered a group of American soldiers, who took you into custody and then back to your unit. Is that correct?"

Gurney struggled with his answer. "We weren't exactly taken into custody, because we did nothing wrong."

49

"We have only your word for that, Gurney. Why did Lieutenant Stiller get executed?"

Gurney shrugged. "I don't know. After we were told to get off our truck, the action was over. I saw the Serge and a couple of other men lying on the ground. I assumed they were dead. Then we were lined up. The leader of the other group accused us of committing treason against the United States of America, punishable by death."

"Punishable by death. That's what he said?"

"Yes, sir. We tried to tell him that he got it all wrong. That's when he ordered Lieutenant Stiller to be executed."

"Why would he do that?"

"I don't know. Maybe because the Lieutenant told the guy to go and fuck himself."

"Or maybe it was because Lieutenant Stiller knew the truth about the shipment of arms and he was guilty of treason."

"I object to that remark!" Gerald Stiller yelled. "My son was not a traitor."

"I warn you, Mr. Morgan," O'Connor said sharply. "Refrain from making inflammatory remarks like that."

"I apologize." Morgan turned back to Gurney. "You admitted you don't remember the name of the man who gave the order. Is that correct?"

"That is correct."

"But you remember that the man gave the order to execute Lieutenant Stiller?"

"Yes, I do. I will never forget that."

"What exactly did he say?"

The soldier wiped his brow. "He said *Take him away. You know what to do*."

"Those were his exact words?"

"Yes, sir."

"Take him away. You know what to do." Morgan smiled grimly. "That doesn't sound like an order to execute someone. What happened next?"

Gurney pointed at Rob. "One of the men, he looked a little like that man, put a gun to the Lieutenant's head and took him behind one of the sheds. Then we heard a shot. He came back alone. Without the Lieutenant."

"So you didn't actually see anyone shoot Lieutenant Stiller?"

Gurney wiped his brow again. He seemed to be sweating profusely. "No, I didn't, but it was obvious. I mean, we all heard the shot, so I assumed…"

"You assumed?" Morgan raised his voice. Suddenly his friendly manner changed. His face took on the expression of a man in rage. "You assumed?" he shouted, pointing a finger at Rob. "You are willing to put the future and possibly the life of a dedicated soldier in jeopardy just because you assumed? You are not even certain if this young man is the one who did the assumed shooting. In fact, there is no evidence that Lieutenant George Stiller is dead. He may have gone AWOL for all we know."

"Never!" bellowed the older Stiller. "My son would never do that! He had no reason to go AWOL because, officially, he wasn't even in the Military anymore. He was part of a covert operation. A secret mission. I can't say anymore."

Morgan looked at him. "Sir, I have deepest respect for your feelings, but I must ask you this…what makes you assume that your son is dead?"

"This man told me." He pointed a shaking finger at Gurney.

Morgan regarded Gurney silently. Then he asked with a mild voice, "What did they promise you, son?"

"I was promised my freedom and honorable discharge from the army."

"Why? Are you now in detention?"

The young soldier nodded.

"What did you do?"

Gurney moved in his seat. Wiping a hand across his face, he said, "I was accused of raping an Iraqi woman." His voice could hardly be heard.

"Accused of raping a woman? Interesting," Morgan said with a loud voice. "That's a serious charge, son. I guess you would do just about anything to make it go away, wouldn't you."

Gurney nodded.

"So you fabricated this ridiculous story, trying to save your neck."

"It's not a fabrication, sir." Gurney lifted his head in protest.

"And I tell you it is because these men you accuse of executing Lieutenant Stiller were never in Iraq at the time this crime is supposed to have taken place. Are you even sure the men you confronted were Americans?"

"They wore US Army uniforms and they spoke English."

"And that makes them American soldiers? Uniforms can be bought and many of the insurgents have a good command of the English language. Tell, me, Private Gurney…are there any other witness to this execution?"

"None who will come forward."

"They can't come forward because they don't exist." Morgan put his hand on Gurney's arm in a show of camaraderie. "I suggest you get yourself a good lawyer and face this rape charge. Take my advice, son, don't use a military lawyer. They don't have the freedom to really fight for you. They're all worried about their future in the Military. If you want a fair trial, get a civilian. Talk to me after this is over."

He turned away and looked at O'Connor. "I'd say you have no case, Colonel. These two men couldn't have committed the crime you are accusing them of because they've been in the US all this time."

"What the hell are you talking about, Morgan!" O'Connor shouted. "I saw them stepping off the bus that brought them from the airport myself. They were on a plane that came from Iraq. I had it checked out."

"You are mistaken, Colonel. They were never in Iraq. You surely must know better than anyone else that every mission is on record somewhere. Are there records of these men having been overseas during the time in question?"

"There are no records because they belong to a unit that doesn't officially exist."

Morgan smiled. "Remember I'm a civilian. I don't know if I want to hear about military units that don't exist. This sounds almost like some kind of conspiracy thing."

"Don't play with words, sir," O'Connor said. "I know who you are. You of all people should know what I'm talking about, Captain Morgan. You've covered your tracks well. You and Colonel Cowley."

"I have no idea what you mean, Colonel. By the way, where is Colonel Cowley?"

"He has been removed from his post and is in custody. He will be dealt with." O'Connor stared at Morgan. "If I were you, sir, I would not be this smug. Somebody will talk and you will all go down, including you. You are not immune."

"Is that a threat, Colonel O'Connor?" Morgan's voice sounded dangerously low. "I hope not and I hope you're not on a witch hunt. You'll never know what might be uncovered."

"I'm warning you, Morgan. This is not over." O'Connor banged his gavel on his desk. "This hearing shall convene at ten hundred tomorrow."

"I have one more question for the witness."

O'Connor glared at Morgan. "It can wait until tomorrow."

"I don't think so." Morgan turned to Gurney. "Did you rape that woman?"

The question seemed to surprise the young soldier. He looked first at O'Connor, then at Morgan. Hesitating, he said, "No, sir, I did not."

"I thought so." Morgan handed him a card. "You need a lawyer badly, son."

Gurney turned the card over in his hand. "I can't afford a high-priced lawyer, sir."

"Don't worry about that. I'll do this one for free."

* * * *

Jeff knew that this might be the day that would determine his and the other men's future.

They were all there. Rob, Harmon, Hung, Armano, and Springer.

They sat on the bench with stoic faces, looking straight ahead. They were soldiers, trained to go into battle without fear. Secure in the craft they had been taught and their ability to adapt to any situation.

And Jeff had no illusions about what they faced here in this room. This was a battle, and the enemy sat behind a desk. An enemy who wanted to smash these soldiers and the unit they belonged to. An enemy who represented the very organization that was supposed to protect them.

The enemy's name was Colonel O'Connor.

A man who owned shares in ADM…American Defense Manufacturing. The same company that sold illegal weapons to insurgents. He may be innocent and not aware of those transactions, but then again, he might be as guilty as hell. If he was, then he was fighting his own battle to save his skin.

He knew about the team's involvement in Iraq. He had to know the shipment of arms never arrived in the hands of the insurgents. Rob had uncovered the orders to hire the mercenaries who accompanied the shipment came from someone in ADM, a Paul Clark. Was he the one who paid the bills?

That left the question as to who hired the soldiers stationed in Iraq. Someone of a higher rank was involved. Someone in Iraq.

The sound of O'Connor's gavel made Jeff look up.

"This hearing will officially commence now. Colonel Cotter will

53

take over from me as head of this investigation."

The man beside O'Connor cleared his throat. "I've been asked by Colonel O'Connor to sit in on this hearing as an independent party. I have no ties to his office or to any of the soldiers stationed on this base. I call the first witness to the stand."

When everyone turned to look back at the opening door, Jeff turned his head also. He stared at the man who walked in.

Colonel Cowley, accompanied by two marines.

They took him to the witness stand and stood beside him after he was seated. His face seemed fallen, pasty. He looked unshaven. Jeff remembered Rob telling him that his father was not well.

"State your name and rank, please," Cotter addressed Cowley.

"My name is Colonel Abraham Cowley." His voice sounded strong, in spite of his appearance.

"Colonel Cowley, you have been accused of heading a subversive unit engaged in illegal activities not sanctioned by the Military or the United States government."

Cowley smiled. "Who accuses me of such a thing?"

"I do, Colonel." O'Connor said.

"Can you provide proof of this preposterous accusation?" Cowley sounded cool and calm.

O'Connor made an impatient gesture. "I have no concrete proof. You know that. Your records have been falsified."

"Do you have proof of that, sir?" Cowley smiled, visibly amused by O'Connor's display of irritation.

"Not yet but I will get proof."

"Well, I suggest you wait until then with your allegations," Cowley suggested. He leaned forward in his seat. He looked at Colonel Cotter. "I am the head of a special branch in Military Intelligence. We operate under cover much of the time and records are kept at a minimum out of necessity to protect my men, but be assured records exist. I get my orders from sources close to the President, some of them from the President himself. Our operations involve national security and cannot be made public, but all operations are authorized by the government." His eyes rested on O'Connor. "If you can produce Top Secret clearance, Colonel, I'll invite you to have a look at our records."

"You know I don't have the necessary clearance," O'Connor blustered.

Cowley smiled smugly. "I know you don't."

"You asked if I had proof," O'Connor said. He pointed at Rob and the others. "I know for a fact these men were in Iraq on a mission. I have sources in Iraq who reported their presence there. In addition, I intercepted a message from a Colonel Settler in Baghdad. It was meant for you, Colonel Cowley. It confirmed what my source already conveyed to me."

"You had no right to read my messages," Cowley said. "They were for my eyes only."

"Well, I did read them." O'Connor's gaze fixed on Jeff. "There was a German with you, a man by the name of Werner Reinhart. You claimed you took him prisoner in Iraq. You promised him his freedom for information."

Jeff shook his head. "I don't recall a man named Reinhart. Where is this man now?"

"I don't know. We released him because he was a civilian, a visitor to this country. He was not a wanted man, and we had no reason to hold him."

"Then he had papers to confirm his legal entry to the US?"

"Yes, he had. He was in possession of a valid passport."

"What did these papers say? Did they mention Iraq? Was there a stamp in his passport that stated he'd been in Iraq?"

"His papers said he was a German National. I don't remember any stamps. What difference does it make?" Colonel Cowley sounded irritated.

Jeff allowed himself a smile. "Then how do you know he came from Iraq?"

"Because you told me that yourself!" O'Connor shouted.

"How could I have brought a man into this country from Iraq if I was never there? You must have misunderstood what I said."

"Are you implying I'm fabricating all of this, Lieutenant?"

"I'm implying nothing, Colonel. I'm at a loss here." Jeff shrugged. "I cannot imagine why you would implicate me of having brought a man from Iraq or of having a man executed in that country. Why would you do that if you have no proof of it having occurred, sir?"

O'Connor's face, usually of little color, turned red as he rose in his seat. Pointing a finger at Jeff, he shouted, "You are accusing a superior officer of lying? Do you know what the penalty is for such a crime?"

Jeff shrugged, trying to show a calmness he didn't feel. When he spoke, he raised his voice a little, "I never said you are lying, sir. I merely stated a question. Is that a crime?"

Colonel Cotter banged his gavel. "Please, everyone stay calm. There will be no slandering remarks at this hearing and no shouting!" He stared at Jeff. "These are serious charges Colonel O'Connor is making against you." He glanced at a sheet of paper he had in front of him. Then he added, "Lieutenant Chartrand."

"Yes, they are serious," Jeff agreed.

Cotter spent a few minutes shuffling through a stack of papers. Then he looked up. "I have your file with me. I need you to clear something up for me. It says here that you were wounded January 29, 1991 while serving in Kuwait. The Military discharged you on March 27, 1991. I have no record that you enlisted again after that. You shouldn't even be here at this hearing. If you have committed a crime you should be in front of a civilian court."

O'Connor leaned over to whisper into Cotter's ear. Cotter nodded and gave Jeff a thoughtful look.

"Why were you hiding in one of the safe houses that belong to the Military?"

"I can clear that up, Colonel Cotter."

Cotter turned his head to look at Cowley. "I'm interested in what you have to say to that, Colonel."

"It is true, Lieutenant Chartrand was not in the Military anymore. Officially. He was a member of my team when the Military honorably discharged him in 1991. Officially, again. But being part of Military Intelligence and being a member of Special Services, in reality he never retired. He was in reserve, his status to be activated when we needed his services. You may or may not be aware that Lieutenant Chartrand's brother Michael was murdered in March of this year. Lieutenant Chartrand was actively involved in the investigation of his brother's murder. We had reason to believe that the murder of Lieutenant Michael Chartrand was connected to his time in Iraq."

"I was not made aware of that. But what has that to do with Lieutenant Jeff Chartrand's hiding in a safe house?"

"In the course of his investigation, Lieutenant Chartrand was involved in a shootout with a Joseph Galliano, a known crime figure in Sacramento. Galliano was killed during this shootout and Chartrand charged with his murder. We believe the charge has no foundation and when Lieutenant Jeff Chartrand asked for our help, we agreed to give it to him. We also agreed to protect him from persecution and lend him the resources of the Military. All of this needed to be done in secrecy."

Colonel Cotter shook his head. "It seems there is much more here than I was told of." He glanced at Colonel O'Connor.

"Lieutenant Chartrand is a wanted criminal, and Colonel Cowley is hiding him from the law. I think he should be in the custody of local law enforcement agencies. Let them handle his case," O'Connor said.

"That is the first logical thing I've heard today." Cotter gave Jeff an inquiring stare. "You will be held in confinement until we have contacted the local authorities and then we will hand you over to them. What happens after is out of our hands. I suggest you get yourself a good lawyer."

Jeff glanced at Rob. "Where the hell is Morgan today?" he whispered.

Rob shrugged his shoulders. "He must be held up somewhere. Don't worry, he'll get you out of this."

"I had hoped my lawyer, Elias Morgan, would be here today," Jeff said to Cotter.

"We were informed he wouldn't be available today…since it's Saturday. He had something else, something more important, planned," O'Connor said, a satisfied smirk playing on his lips. "Not that it would make any difference."

"It wouldn't," Cotter agreed. "This is not a matter of the Military." He looked at Cowley. "Colonel Cowley, as far as you and your men are concerned, I will have to give the matter a closer look and then I will determine how we shall proceed. I need to speak with my superiors in Washington to help me make a decision." He banged his gavel against the desktop. "This hearing is adjourned until further notice."

Jeff turned to look at the two armed marines approaching him. He didn't object when they led him away. He walked between them with mixed feelings and was happy in a way to be back in his cell. There was nothing for him to do but wait now.

Chapter Six

Next morning, the same two marines marched him across the compound and into the mess hall for breakfast. When he stood in line for his food, he noticed Rob and the other members of the team where already there. Nobody stopped him when he walked over to their table and took the seat next to Rob.

"How are they treating you, Lieutenant?" Harmon asked.

"Can't complain." Jeff chuckled. "Although I can think of better places to be than in a cell all by myself."

"I agree," Harmon said.

"How about you guys?"

"We're okay." Springer glanced at the armed soldiers by the door. "We could easily take them out and escape."

"We could, but then what?" Rob asked. "Like I told the Lieutenant, O'Connor's got nothing on us. He's bluffing."

"Perhaps not on us, but what about the Lieutenant?" Hung's almond eyes studied Jeff. "They say you shot Galliano. Is there any truth to that?"

Jeff nodded. "It was either him or me."

"The man deserved to die," Springer said.

"He certainly did," Jeff said grimly. "I don't feel sorry it happened, especially since I just found out that he was responsible for my brother's murder."

"I don't believe you have anything to worry about, Lieutenant," Harmon said with conviction.

"Thank you guys for the encouraging words." Jeff smiled. It was good to have some friends in this hostile world. He knew these men genuinely cared for him as a person. Spending time with them on the mission in Iraq had gained him their respect. He thought about Rob's suggestion he should take over the Colonel's job. A job he wasn't sure he really wanted. Looking at the faces of the six men, he knew he'd feel honored to be their team leader.

He thought about Colonel Cowley. Rob was right the man didn't seem well. It was only a matter of time before he had to resign from his post. Who would replace him? Somebody the men didn't know? A man they would not trust? It could mean the end of Grey Ops.

As if reading Jeff's thoughts, Springer said, "The Colonel didn't look too good."

"No, he didn't," Rob said. It was clear from the tone of his voice that he was concerned. "At least we know that he is still alive."

"They must have kept him in some dark hole somewhere, those bastards," Harmon growled angrily.

"By *they* you mean O'Connor and his cohort?" Springer asked.

"Of course. Who else?" Harmon scowled. "He wants to disband Grey Ops, discredit the Colonel and feed us to the wolves."

"Why?" Jeff asked. "What does he have against Colonel Cowley? Or, for that matter, against Grey Ops?"

"As far as I know, he's investigating corruption in the Military. Rumors have it, he is seeking a seat in the Senate," Rob explained. "He's a politician. He doesn't really care about us personally."

"I don't think he likes me," Jeff said with a chuckle.

"And he seems to hate Colonel Cowley for some reason," Armano added. "Why?"

"That goes back a long way," Rob said. "He and Colonel Cowley went to the Academy together. I don't exactly know what went down there."

"In other words, it is a personal vendetta he has against Colonel Cowley." Hung shook his head. "It must have been something pretty bad if he carried it around with him all these years."

"I can't tell you what it is because I don't know," Rob said. His eyes scanned the room. "I'm telling you this in confidence. The Lieutenant and I have been doing some investigating and we've uncovered some interesting things. The righteous Colonel O'Connor owns a large portion in American Defense Manufacturing. We have evidence that ADM is selling arms to Iraq."

"Wow!" Harmon let out a low whistle. "Does that mean O'Connor is behind these illegal arms deals?"

"We don't have proof of that yet," Rob cautioned.

"Son of a bitch!" Springer cursed. "Now this whole thing is beginning to make sense. He knows we were the ones responsible for the last deal to go sour. The only way to save his skin is to get rid of Colonel

Cowley and us. This is more than politics, my friend. He's fighting for his life."

"That's right. We have to tread very carefully. The only way to save our skins is to expose him. We can do that only if we stay free." Rob's voice was barely a whisper. "I don't know if he has interrogated any of you, but remember this, we were never in Iraq. The mission never took place. Deny everything. He might be trying to break us individually. Don't give in to anything he promises. He will never keep his word."

Hung made a deep sound in his throat. "I feel almost insulted, Rob. You know us better than that. We are brothers. Blood brothers. We will always be true to each other." He made a fist and laid it on the table. "We few, we happy few, we band of brothers."

The others put their fists on his and murmured, "Forever and a day."

Jeff smiled grimly. He recognized the words, written by William Shakespeare over four hundred years ago. They had not lost their magic.

We band of brothers!

He envied them. He was part of the team now, but not the way they were. It would take much more than one mission to be one of them.

Finishing his breakfast, he looked up at the guards who came to take him back to his cell.

"My heart is true as steel," he said to the men still sitting at the table, quoting a line from A Midsummer Night's Dream. They looked at him, nodded, their faces somber. He knew they understood the meaning of the words.

They knew he would never betray them, either.

As the guards accompanied him across the compound, he saw the two black cars parked in front of the stockade but didn't give them any thoughts. Only when he reached the door to his cell and saw the four men with dark glasses and in suits standing by the door, he knew that they were waiting for him.

"Jeffrey Chartrand?" one of them asked.

He gave the speaker a tight smile. "You know who I am. What can I do for you?"

"Agent Frank Boychuk from Homeland Security," the man said, flashing a wallet. "We are here to take you into custody. Please, come with us."

"I'm not free to go with you. As you can see, the Military has put a claim on me. You might want to take it up with Colonel O'Connor."

"No need to, sir. You have been released by the Military and handed over to us."

"What for?"

"Please, don't make it difficult, sir. You are on the wanted list of every law enforcement agency in the country. We are arresting you for suspected dealings with enemies of the United States of America. That is only one of the charges. Shall I go on?"

Jeff was getting tired of this whole game. He waved a hand in dismissal. "Spare me the details, Agent Boychuk. How's MacKay these days?"

"He is fine, sir. Now come with us, peacefully."

Jeff looked at the two marines who stood waiting. "You heard the man. If you have no objections, I'll be going away with these fine gentlemen."

One of the marines nodded. "That is okay with us, sir. We've been informed by Colonel Cotter."

"How about Colonel O'Connor?"

"It is Colonel Cotter who made the decision, sir." The two marines turned as one and marched away.

Boychuk chuckled. "Those guys are like robots. You'll have much more fun with us, Chartrand."

Resigning to his fate, Jeff walked with them out of the building again and climbed into the backseat of one of the cars. Boychuk joined him in the backseat, while another of the agents took the seat beside the driver.

None of the agents had drawn any weapons, but Jeff had noticed the bulges in their jackets.

The first of the cars sped away. The car Jeff was in followed at a slower pace.

"Where are you taking me?" Jeff asked, trying to make conversation. It never hurt to be friendly with people who might be in a position to harm him.

"You'll see," Boychuk answered laconically. "And now please be silent. I'm not in the mood for conversation."

Jeff noticed the agent in the passenger's seat watching the side mirror.

"I think we are being followed," the agent said after watching the mirror for a while.

Boychuk turned his head and looked out of the rear view window. "I don't see anything suspicious."

"The delivery van a few cars back, in the right lane," the other agent said. "I've been watching it and noticed it hanging back, letting other cars pass. When we took the side street a couple of miles back, that van did the same. I don't like it."

"I think you're paranoid, Keller." Boychuk settled back in his seat. "Nobody even knows we're here, except for MacKay."

"And those guys on the military base," Keller insisted.

"They are the ones who called us. They wanted to get rid of this guy, not keep him." Boychuk sounded irritated. "Just relax, Keller."

They stopped at a red light. Jeff saw a black windowless van pulling up beside them. Then things happened quickly.

Two men wearing balaclavas jumped out of the back of the van. One of them ran around the car, while the other one calmly walked up to the passenger's side. Before Jeff could utter a warning, the masked man aimed his gun at the agent in the passenger's seat and shot him in the head.

Jeff heard the shattering of glass, registered the second shot that killed the driver. He reached for the handle of his door, saw the gun aimed at Boychuk, heard the shot. Then he ripped open the doors but stopped when the gunman on his side pointed his gun at him.

"Get into the van!" the masked man ordered him with a raspy voice.

He came around the open door, shoved the gun into Jeff's side. "Now, move!"

Jeff threw a glance into the car, saw all three agents slumped in their seats. Boychuk's face was turned toward him, his eyes were open and staring and his lips were pulled into the parody of a smile. The small hole in his forehead looked like a neat red spot. Blood sprayed from the back of his skull, painting the seat with a crimson pattern.

"Move!" the man behind him gave him a shove.

Jeff stumbled toward the van. The other masked gunman joined his companion and they pushed him into the back of the van and locked it behind him.

Jeff sprawled onto the floor as the vehicle lurched and began moving. He groped around in the darkness to find a hold but gave up and pressed himself tightly against the hard floorboards to keep from rolling around.

Boychuk's grinning visage filled his mind. It brought back the memory of Michael's murder. He could still see him sitting on the couch, his eyes staring into nothingness, like a man in a deep trance. The only thing that had spoiled that image was the dark hole between his eyes.

He felt sudden sadness. He did not know these three men who had died in a matter of minutes. They had families. Loved ones who would be mourning their deaths.

He became angry with the ones who had done this. They had ripped families apart by their senseless act, just to get him. He didn't believe for one minute that this was a rescue mission. His life was in danger; he had no illusions about that.

He wondered why they had not shot him also, and not for the first time since his brother's death, he asked himself what had spawned all this violence.

What did you do, Michael, to cause all of this? Why were you murdered in the first place? How many people will still have to die before this is over?

He lay in the darkness, pressed against the floorboards. The vehicle finally stopped. He squinted against the bright light flooding in when the doors opened.

"Out!" one of the masked men ordered him.

He thought about resisting, trying to flee, but when he counted five men with drawn guns, all of them aimed at him, he gave up that thought. Before he could look around, one of the men put a dark hood over his head and shut out the light.

He staggered between them as they led him to an unknown destination. "What do you want from me?" he asked.

The sharp pain from a punch into his kidneys made him cry out involuntarily. He wanted to strike back but resisted the urge. They had the advantage. He could only lash out blindly, hoping to hit someone. He knew he'd probably be dead in moments. If not dead, then beaten badly.

There was only one thing to do and that was to wait until his time came.

From the echo of their footsteps, he deducted that they were in a large room, empty perhaps of any furnishings. Possibly an abandoned warehouse or a store. He didn't think he was in a military compound. He would have heard the sounds of vehicles and men, soldiers.

There was no doubt in his mind about his captors being soldiers. Possibly not active but definitely ex-military. The operation had gone smoothly, well planned. Efficient.

Who would want him captured?

They stopped. He stumbled when someone pushed him forward.

Then he heard the closing of a door behind him.

Luckily, they had not bound his arms. He reached up to take off the hood. Looking around, he saw the open doors of stalls with toilets and a couple of sinks. He also noticed a number of urinals on one wall.

This looked like a public washroom…an abandoned public washroom. The floor was filthy, there were stains on the urinals and the two sinks looked rusty, unused. When he walked over to one of the sinks and opened the tap, no water came out of it. Definitely an abandoned washroom.

He grinned at his image in the only mirror. It was cracked and covered with grime, but he could still see his face. "At least I can take a piss if I need to," he said to his counterpart in the mirror.

His image mocked his grin, mouthed the words with him.

It wasn't completely dark inside the room. A small, barred window high above in the back wall let in enough light to let him see the dirt on the floor, the dust on the fixtures, and the metal barriers dividing the stalls. He walked over to one of the porcelain toilets and looked inside. They were stained yellow from the rust in the water that had evaporated long ago.

He shrugged. If he needed to, he could use one of the toilets, but he hoped that would not be necessary. Without water to flush, it would not be pleasant.

When he heard the door opening, he turned but stayed where he was. Two men, weapons drawn, entered the room. Neither of them wore masks.

That was not a good sign.

Both men were big, at least as bulky as he. One probably outweighed him by twenty pounds. Neither of them was fat. Even without their weapons, they would not be easy to overcome. It may even end up fatal for him if he tried.

"Lieutenant Jeff Chartrand," the larger man said, "I hope we didn't inconvenience you by bringing you here?"

The other one laughed. Jeff noticed that his two front teeth were missing. "Are the accommodations to your liking?" he asked. He spoke with a slight lisp when his tongue hit the front of his mouth where two teeth should be.

Too bad I wasn't the one who broke them.

He gave them a cold look. "What do you want from me?"

"The last time you asked that question it earned you a kick in the kidneys," the one with the missing teeth said.

"I assume you were the one who hit me?"

The man grinned. It didn't make him appear any more compassionate. "You're a smart guy, Lieutenant, to figure that out."

"Maybe I can pay you back some time," Jeff said.

"I doubt that. You see you're not going anywhere."

His companion threw him a warning glance. "You talk too much."

Jeff didn't have to guess how this little adventure would end. "You still haven't answered my question," he said.

"We will ask the questions, Lieutenant." He pulled a small device out of his breast pocket. An electronic recording device. He smiled. "We can end this whole thing very quickly. It is up to you. Just so there are no misunderstanding later about what you said, I will record our conversation. I hope you don't mind?" He gave Jeff a mocking chuckle.

Jeff shrugged. "Go ahead. Ask away."

"Where you in Iraq between June eleven and June twenty-six?"

The question came unexpected. "What if I was?"

"I take that as a yes. Did you and the team known as Grey Ops thwart an arms deal between a group of American soldiers and Iraqi freedom fighters?"

"I never said I was in Iraq, which means I could not have interfered with an illegal arms deal."

"Are you denying your involvement in the killing of a number of Iraqi freedom fighters?"

Jeff leaned against the metal door of the stall. "I don't understand why you are asking me these questions. What is your interest in what I did in the month of June?"

The big man came closer. His expression was one of annoyance and suppressed anger. "My brother was murdered during that incident. Maybe you'll remember him. His name was George Stiller. Lieutenant George Stiller."

Jeff didn't answer immediately. Looking at the face of the big man, he saw the resemblance. The man was unshaven, that's why he hadn't noticed the likeness right away. He shrugged. "I'm sorry to hear about your brother, but I had nothing to do with his death. I was never in Iraq."

"You are lying!" Stiller said between clenched teeth. "I have it from a man who witnessed my brother's execution. He was there and he swore that you were there also."

"Then he's lying. I was never there." Jeff moved slightly forward, away from the stalls. He casually lifted his hands, his body tensed as he readied himself for an attack.

But it never came. The big man glared at him. "I'm going to give you an hour to think about it and then I'll be back." He turned. Without a backward glance, he stalked out of the room. His companion threw Jeff a look of contempt, and then he followed Stiller.

Jeff relaxed and sighed. This definitely didn't feel promising. The two men had not attempted to disguise themselves. One of them had even given part of his name.

They could never let him walk out of here alive. They meant to kill him.

He looked at the small window and ruled it out as his way of escaping. Even without the thick iron bars it would have been too small for a man of his size. Besides, he would either need a ladder to reach it or have suction cups on his hands and feet to climb the wall.

They came for him again after an hour had passed.

This time there were four men. Two men covered him with their guns, while the other two tied his hands together behind his back with tie wraps. Then they prodded him and told him to move.

He walked between the two men into a large cavern-like room. Remnants of shelves on the walls confirmed that this had once been a store. Broken and twisted pieces of metal, rusted shelves and cross pieces lay strewn across the ripped-up floor. A layer of dust and dirt covered everything. It rose into the air as the men walked across the grimy floor, leaving their footprints behind.

They took him to a metal chair and told him to take a seat. When he sat, one of them wrapped his body with ropes. Then they walked away again.

Jeff tried to break his bonds but found they had done a good job of rendering him immobile. His legs were tied to the chair, making it impossible to move, even with the chair. The only thing he could do was maybe topple his body to the side, but that would have made no sense. Therefore, he just sat and waited.

After about half an hour, they came back.

"Well?" Stiller said. "Have you given the matter some thought?"

"There is nothing to think about," Jeff said. "I'm sticking to my story. I was not in Iraq during the time you said I was."

Stiller kicked him in the chest with his booted foot, throwing him and his chair backward.

Jeff suppressed a moan when the pain shot through his chest. His head hit the hard floor and sent another stab of pain into his brain.

Two of the men lifted him and his chair and pushed him back into the vacated spot.

"How's your memory now?" Stiller asked, his face a cold mask of fury.

"The same," Jeff said, clenching his teeth, ready for another kick.

"Let me repeat the question. Did you and the team known as Grey Ops prevent the shipment of arms to freedom fighters in Iraq on the night of Friday, the twenty-second of June?"

Jeff gave a loud sigh. "You must be deaf. I told you before, I did not, since I was not in Iraq at that particular time."

"And I told you I have a reliable witness," Stiller snarled. He came close to Jeff and, with a casual swing, backhanded him.

Jeff felt the blood trickling down his cheek where Stiller's ring ripped it open. He tried to shut out the sudden pain and managed not to cry out.

Stiller stepped back and looked at one of the watching men. "Maybe you can talk some sense into our guest."

The man grinned and punched his fists into his open hand. "I could give it a try," he said and, without warning, he smashed his fist against the side of Jeff's head.

This time Jeff let out a loud moan. His head rang from the punch. He shook it, trying to still the sudden ringing in his ears. He thought he might lose consciousness, was almost sorry when he didn't.

"Ready to talk?" Stiller asked.

Jeff stared at him through a red haze. "I can't tell you anything except what I already told you, but you refuse to hear," he said. His voice sounded strange in his own ears.

"Untie him!" Stiller said to the other men.

Two of them followed his order.

When Jeff was free, Stiller told him to stand up.

Jeff tried and almost collapsed when a wave of dizziness made him stagger, but he managed to stand straight. Defiantly, he looked at the big man in front of him.

"Defend yourself," Stiller said, throwing a punch at Jeff.

His reflexes were slow. He lifted both of his hands to block the punch. Then he moved back, barely avoiding another blow. The next one hit him in the belly. He registered the pain, bent forward as his body acted in reflex. This whole thing had a dreamlike quality to it. It felt unreal. He thought of himself as an observer, not a participant.

He kicked with his foot, felt it connect. Then he took a blow to the head. Somehow, it seemed to bring him back to reality. Shaking his head to clear it, he fell into a fighting stance, his fist shot out, found his opponent's wide chin. He heard Stiller utter a loud curse and blocked another punch.

Dancing back, he didn't quite avoid the other man's fist. It hit him on the side of his face, intensifying the pain of his cut cheek.

The other man was relentless, as he threw punch after punch. Jeff stumbled, unable to avoid the barrage to his upper body and his head.

Lights flashed through his brain and then his consciousness slipped away.

Chapter Seven

Get up, Darling, dance with me.

She whirled away, her long legs kicking up, exposing her naked buttocks. He caught a glimpse of her shaved pubis. Laughing, she came back into his arms, green eyes flashing, her auburn hair swirling around her freckled face.

Dance with me.

Nicole. What are you doing here?

Dancing, my darling, dancing.

He reached for her. She laughed with a hollow sound. Staring into the empty sockets where her eyes should be, he screamed and stumbled back.

Dance with me.

Her foot caught him in the chest as she lashed out. Then her fist smashed into his face. Reeling from the pain, he held up his hands and tried to protect his nose.

The horror that had once been his lovely Nicole kicked him repeatedly, until he lay whimpering on the floor.

The pain! The terrible pain.

I love you, he cried.

She twirled on long legs.

When she turned to look back at him, she had changed. Instead of Nicole, George Stiller stared at him. Blood oozed from a hole in his forehead.

You killed me, he said with an accusing voice.

You deserved to die. You betrayed your country.

Stiller laughed and kicked with a booted foot.

It hurts. My head hurts. My chest hurts when I breathe.

It's just a nightmare. Wake up.

Wake up.

Jeff opened his eyes, looked around and moaned when the movement sent stabs of pain through his head. His face burned.

Wake up!

He tried to sit and fell back as a wave of nausea made him dizzy. I'm still dreaming, he thought. He lay there, staring at the barred window. The bright disk of the full moon shone through the dirty pane, filling the room with an eerie light.

Then he remembered.

This was not a nightmare. This was reality.

He winced when he tried to take a deep breath. His lungs seemed to be on fire. Discovering that his hands weren't bound anymore, he probed his chest with one hand, nearly cried out when he touched his left side. *I think I've got some broken ribs.* His fingers moved up to his face. He felt the crusted blood that had soaked his beard. But at least his nose wasn't broken. His lips felt swollen and cracked. Aware of his parched throat, he knew he was on the verge of becoming de-hydrated. He hadn't had anything to eat and drink since breakfast.

He managed to sit up, waited until the wave of nausea abated, and then he rose to his feet. Swaying, he stood for a moment. *I need to take a piss.* Stumbling to the urinal, he steadied himself against the metal wall of the stall next to it. He felt like vomiting but suppressed the urge.

I can't lose any more liquid.

He strained his ears but didn't hear anyone. When he walked over to the door, he found it locked. Banging his fists against the door didn't produce any results.

Why was he still alive?

He knew one of his captors was George Stiller's brother. He had motive to kill him, but that was not the reason they had kidnapped him. How had they known about his whereabouts at that particular time? Somebody must have tipped them off. Somebody who knew about him.

He remembered Stiller saying he was in possession of reliable information about Jeff's time in Iraq. That could only mean that one or more of the soldiers involved in that arms deal were back in the States, like Raymond Gurney. He was one of the men accompanying the arms shipment, but he didn't recognized Jeff because of his red beard.

He could think of only one other man who could have leaked information.

Colonel O'Connor.

Aside from Colonel Cotter and the two marines, he was the only other person who knew that Homeland Security had picked up Jeff. He ruled out Cotter and the marines. That left only O'Connor.

Jeff slid to the floor and leaned his back against the wall. It didn't appear that anyone was outside. He might as well get some rest. He had no illusions about what waited for him in the morning, and he didn't look forward to the end of the night.

He slept fitfully, his dreams filled with memories of Kuwait, of trudging through dry sand, fighting sandstorms, inhaling dust through a burning throat. The fire in his lungs. He awoke and coughed, his throat raw and crying for liquid.

What's your name, soldier?

George Stiller. Ex-marine. Fuck you.

Take him away. You know what to do.

He opened his eyes, disoriented. Stared at the barred window. The moon had moved, wasn't visible through the small window, but its eerie light still filled the room.

His chest ached with every breath he took.

You did the right thing, Jeff.

He stared in horror at the blood oozing out of her shoulder. Kalila. Beautiful Kalila. Please, don't die. She looked at him with her dark haunting eyes. Lifting a slim hand, she touched his cheek. I love you, Jeff.

Her eyes changed shape. Her arms reached up, pulled him into her embrace. He felt her naked skin warm against his, felt the pressure of her slim thighs on his hips. Her moans of pleasure sounded like music in his ears.

I love you.

And I love you, Connie.

He sat up with a start, cried out involuntarily when the pain raced through his chest. The light falling through the window had changed. He could see red streaks against the dark sky.

It must be close to morning.

He drifted off into sleep again, despite the pain in his side.

He woke when someone poured a bucket of water over his head. Sputtering, he stared into the face of the guy with the two teeth missing.

"Had a restful night, I hope?" The man grinned and kicked him in the side.

Jeff groaned, tried to move out of the way. Frantically running his tongue across his lips, he swallowed a few drops of the water running down his face, not caring if it was clean or not. "I'm thirsty," he said. His voice came out in a croak.

"I just gave you some water. Lick if off the floor," his captor said with a cruel twist of his mouth. He grabbed Jeff under one shoulder. "Now, get up!"

Jeff rose painfully to his feet. Stumbling out of the door, he let himself be propelled forward. The chair was still where it had been the day before. He counted only three men waiting for him. Stiller stood wide legged with his arms crossed. Jeff noticed with satisfaction that his chin looked bruised.

"My oh my, look at the tough Lieutenant Chartrand now," Stiller said, mockingly. "I hope you gave your predicament some thought because my patience is running out. Either way, this whole charade will be ending today. We can make it fast or drag it out. I have all day."

"I have no plans to go anywhere," Jeff said defiantly. He even managed a small chuckle.

"Tie him up!" Stiller ordered his men.

When Jeff was securely tied up, Stiller pulled out his gun and put it against Jeff's head. "I could finish you off right now, Chartrand, take all the pain away or I can add more to your pain."

"Either way you'll kill me, right?"

Stiller's smile showed almost pity. "I can't let you live, Chartrand, you know that. But that is not the point here. If you tell me what I want to hear, you'll die quickly. That is the least I can do for your co-operation, even though you don't deserve it after having my brother executed. However, I'm not a monster." He paused. "On the other hand, should I not like what you'll tell me, I promise you, your death will be slow and painful. Very painful. My buddy Steven here loves his job. He used to interrogate prisoners in Iraq and he usually got results. They all confessed."

"Good for him. You want me to give him a medal for torturing prisoners?" Jeff said sarcastically.

"You won't be so smug when I'm through with you, you son of a bitch," the guy with the missing front teeth snarled. He walked up to Jeff and cuffed him across the face.

Jeff let out an involuntary groan when he felt the wound in his cheek opening up again.

"Enough," Stiller said. "Now, what can you tell me, Chartrand?"

Jeff squinted at him. "I forgot the question. Can you repeat it again?"

Stiller shook his head. "Go ahead, play your games. You can't be that stupid."

Jeff grimaced. "Maybe your blows to my head gave me amnesia. I can't seem to remember a thing."

"Maybe this will jog your memory." Stiller punched him with his fist.

Jeff felt the blood running from a split brow and he blinked when it trickled into his eye. He clenched his teeth. "Nope. That doesn't to do anything."

The ringing in his ears seemed to have intensified. He didn't know how much he could still take. "What was it you wanted to know?"

"All right. I'll humor you. Were you and your team known as Grey Ops in Iraq between June eleven and June twenty-six of this year?"

"I don't recall ever hearing about the Grey Ops. Who are they?"

"What the fuck! You must really think I'm an idiot!" Stiller cursed and waved his gun around. He pointed it at Jeff. "I feel like ending this and putting a bullet into your fucking brain, but I've got orders."

"I knew there had to be somebody else involved besides you four clowns," Jeff said. "You're not smart enough to have pulled this off by yourself. Anyone I know?"

Stiller didn't answer. He glared at Jeff with an angry expression in his face and eyes, like a man gone crazy and on the verge of losing control.

"Just finish him off already," one of the other men said. "He won't be talking. I know his type. These spooks are all alike. You'll never break him."

"Oh, shut up, Cavanaugh! I don't need your stupid comments."

"Don't tell me to shut up, Stiller! I have better thing to do than stand here all day and watch you get off beating another guy to death."

Cavanaugh.

Jeff filed the name away. He may never get the chance to reveal it, but he was still alive. As long as he was alive, he had hope. Maybe they would start fighting among each other and leave, giving him time to recover a little. A chance to escape might suddenly open up.

"You're right, Cavanaugh. I'm getting tired of this whole mess." He walked up to Jeff and grabbed him by the hair. "I gave you a chance to explain yourself. I might even have let you live, but you dug your own grave."

He stepped back and nodded to the guy with the missing teeth. "He's all yours, Steven. Maybe you can convince him to confess. I don't really care anymore. Do what you want. Put him into the incinerator when it's done and make sure you clean up the mess. Leave no traces, understand?"

"Don't worry, Stiller. I've done it before. Nobody will ever find any evidence he was ever here."

Jeff watched Stiller and two of the men walking away.

"Well, it's just you and me now, big guy," Steven said, rubbing his hands.

"I think I'll have to go to the can," Jeff said.

"What?" Steven broke into loud laughter. "You are too much. You're about to die and you want to go for a crap?"

"Better than crapping into my pants, isn't it?" Jeff tried to smile. "Look at it this way, at least you won't have to handle the mess I'd be making."

"All right." He gave Jeff a dubious look. "You're not thinking of making a run for it, are you?"

Jeff chuckled. "Tied to a chair?"

"Don't act stupid. I'll have to untie you."

"I'd appreciate it."

Steven bent and began undoing the rope. "I'll be watching you," he warned. "I'll shoot you down like a rabid dog if you try anything."

"Don't worry. I can barely stand." Jeff wriggled his fingers to put some circulation back into them and rose carefully. His feet felt surprisingly steady and he walked toward the washroom.

"At least be descent enough and give me some privacy," he said when he stood in front of the door that led into the washroom.

Steven shrugged. "There is no way out of there. Just go in and do your business. Don't take all day, though."

"Thanks, buddy." Jeff pretended to sway and leaned against the door. He smiled apologetically. "My legs are a little weak. It'll take me a while just to walk to the can. Have a little patience."

"All right. Just go already."

Jeff opened the door and closed it behind him. Once inside the room, he looked around frantically for some kind of weapon. This was it. If he let Steven tie him up again, he was done for.

He looked at the metal crosspieces that held the stalls together. Working as fast he could without screaming when he made a wrong move and the pain threatened to overcome him, he managed to loosen one of the struts. He swung it experimentally and was satisfied that it might just do the trick.

Steven banged his fist against the door. "Are you finally done in there?"

"I'm good, but I seem to have a cramp in my leg. I can't get off the stall," Jeff called.

"What the hell! Are you asking me to come and get you?"

"If you could."

"Fuck this!" Steven cursed.

Jeff waited by the door, his arm raised, the piece of metal in his hand. There was no room for mistakes. His first strike had to put Steven out of action; otherwise, he might as well say his last prayer. He would never be able to go against Steven. Even though he was slightly smaller than Jeff, he was rested and without pain.

The door opened and Steven walked in.

Jeff swung his primitive weapon with all his might. He smashed the metal strut against Steven's temple. The big man kept on walking and Jeff readied himself to swing his weapon again, when Steven came to a dead stop. His body folded, and he collapsed like a rag doll. His gun clattered onto the floor.

Jeff rushed to pick it up and aimed it at the immobile body on the floor.

Steven didn't move. Jeff prodded him with his foot, but the man lay still. When Jeff looked into his face, he noticed the slack expression. Then he saw the open eyes and knew the man was dead. A quick check of his pulse confirmed it.

Jeff straightened out and took a deep breath. His chest ached, but he didn't care. He was alive and one of his captures dead. That was all that counted at the moment. He stuck the gun into his belt and went through Steven's pockets. He was almost ecstatic when he found a cell phone.

Whom could he phone? Not Rob. He was probably still in custody.

He could think of only one man who might be able to get him out fast and hide him again, if necessary.

Morgan.

He phoned information since he did not know Morgan's phone number. His head was still buzzing and he had nothing to write it down, but he managed to remember the number information gave him.

When he dialed the number, he prayed Morgan was in the office. He was lucky. When the secretary told him Mr. Morgan was busy, he spoke with urgency, trying to make her understand he could not wait, "This is an emergency. Tell him Lieutenant Jeff Chartrand is in trouble. I need to talk to him now. It is a matter of life and death."

"Just one moment, please. I'll see what I can do."

While he talked to the secretary, he walked through the building, looking for an exit. He found it and squinted at the bright sun that greeted him outside. As expected, he had been in an abandoned store. There was no traffic outside on the street. Most of the buildings looked abandoned. He had no idea where he was.

When the secretary came back on, she said, "Mr. Morgan will talk to you now, Lieutenant Chartrand."

"Chartrand?" Morgan's voice sounded stunned.

"I need your help, Morgan," Jeff said. He was looking around to find his bearing.

"What the hell happened, Chartrand? I thought you were dead."

Jeff chuckled into the phone. "No, not quite, but almost."

"It was all over the news. Three agents killed in cold blood in the middle of the day. Did you have anything to do with that?"

"No. Listen, there is no time to explain. Just get me out of here. Fast. I don't know how much time I have. By the way, I'm in bad shape. Bring some painkillers."

There was a slight pause on the other end. "Where are you?"

"I was in an abandoned store, but I'm outside now. On the street. There are a lot of vacant old warehouses all over the place. Just a minute, I can see a street sign." Jeff nearly ran to the street corner. When he read the name on the sign, Morgan said, "Give me a moment, I'll search for it. There. I found it."

"Can you send someone?"

"Stay where you are and I'll have somebody there within thirty minutes."

"How will I recognize him?"

"This person will be in a yellow corvette."

"All right. I'll wait. Thanks." He shoved the phone into his pocket and headed for the nearest building. He couldn't take the chance and wait on the street. Stiller and the others might just decide to come back and check up on Steven.

He settled down just inside the building. It smelled of decay and urine. It was probably used by vagrants and drug users. There was nobody in it now and he was glad he didn't have to explain himself to anyone who might challenge his presence.

It was hot outside, but sitting in the shade of the building made it bearable. His whole body ached and he felt like vomiting. He could hear his stomach complaining. His throat burned from lack of moisture. Right now he was running on pure adrenalin. It wouldn't last long before he'd collapse from exhaustion.

I should have told Morgan to send something to drink. A sandwich would have been nice.

He could hear the noise of traffic in the distance, and then he heard the rumbling of a car's motor. That had to be the corvette. He saw the yellow shape coming down the main road and he walked out of the building, looking around, making sure no one else was following the corvette.

He waved and waited until the car stopped. Looking inside, he was surprised to see a woman behind the wheel. She looked somewhat familiar.

The window was down and she said, "Get in. I was told you are in a hurry."

He opened the door, grimaced when he tried to squeeze his bulk into the low seat. "You have no idea how much in a hurry."

Her eyes widened when she saw him. "Good god," she uttered. "What happened to you?"

"I've had a run-in with some people who didn't like me."

"I'll say. Did you get robbed?"

"No." He sighed, happy to be sitting. "Please, just drive. I will explain everything to Morgan. Did you get instructions where to take me?"

"To my place." She smiled when she saw his astonished look. "It's the safest place for you to be. No one will suspect you there."

"Do you know who I am?" he asked.

She nodded, while gunning the motor. "I'm Jenny Morgan. Elias is my father. I am a private investigator. I work mostly for my father's firm, but I also do freelance work."

He remembered now why she looked familiar. The picture on Morgan's desk. Not of her but probably of her mother. "Aren't you a little too young for that kind of work?"

She laughed, shaking her dark hair out of her eyes. "I'm older than I look. Is there anything else you'd like to add?"

"Like what?"

"That I'm a woman?"

Jeff chuckled, and then he moaned and put his hand on his chest, trying to shut out the pain.

She glanced at him. "Are you in pain?"

"Only when I laugh. You didn't by any chance bring any painkillers, did you?"

"There was no time. I'll have some at home. Can you hold on until then?"

"I guess I'll have to. Can you drive faster than this? I thought corvette drivers always race."

"I'm not that fast." She threw him a quick glance. "In many ways but not all."

He smiled, wondering what she meant. Right now, he was in no mood for any friendly bantering, even with a beautiful woman. Every breath he took sent liquid fire through his side. He could barely see out of his left eye. It was hidden under a puffed-up brow and his lips felt as if they were three times their size.

"Do you mind if I rest a little?" he asked, suddenly feeling weak.

"Go ahead. Sleep if you must. My place is still another twenty minutes away."

Chuckling a little, he closed his eyes, thankful for the opportunity to finally relax. What irony, to feel safe inside a speeding corvette driven by a woman.

Chapter Eight

She helped him out of the car. His limbs had stiffened up from sitting for so long.

"Can you walk?" He detected the concern in her voice.

"I'll manage," he said, leaning on her. She was not a big woman, but he felt the hardness of muscles where he touched her.

This was not some soft party girl, even though she looked like one.

She lived in an apartment on the second floor in a building with tight security. They took the elevator from the underground parking garage. Even the garage was secure. No car would ever be allowed to enter without a pass. Only tenants of the building were in possession of a pass.

"Nice place," he commented when they stepped into her apartment.

"It is home," she said, smiling. "Sit down over there on the chesterfield. I want to take a picture of you."

"Why?"

"For possible future use. One never knows when a picture will come in handy." She helped him to the chesterfield. Looking at him, she shook her head. "You sure look quite a mess. Whoever worked you over did a good job."

"How about giving me those painkillers before you take pictures?" He sank into the soft material, noticed it was leather. It looked expensive. No imitation here. Everything in her apartment looked expensive. The pictures on the walls; no prints, all original oils. The statue of a man and a woman embracing in the corner was exquisite.

"You seem to be doing well," he said.

"Can't complain. Now wait until I get your pills."

He watched her walking away. She was slim, tall, maybe five seven or eight, with a walk that conveyed grace and strength. And she reeked of sensuality. She wore tight white pants that ended below her knees. Her calves were well formed, her ankles thin. He spotted a picture of her in a gi, with a black belt. It didn't come as a surprise.

"Here we are." She came out of the bathroom, went to a cupboard and took out a glass, filled it with water.

He took the pill from her, put into his mouth and washed it down with the water. "Is this water safe to drink?" he asked.

She chuckled and shrugged. "I hope so. I've been drinking it without any ill effects." She watched him empty the glass. "Want some more?"

"No, maybe later. I'd appreciate something to eat, if you have. My belly is growling and calling for food."

"Let me take the pictures first. Then I'll make you a sandwich. All right?"

He nodded, winced when a flash of pain raced from his neck down his spine. He could only see with one eye now. His other one was swollen shut. He was afraid to look into a mirror.

She got a small digital camera and snapped some pictures.

"You want me to smile?" he asked in an attempt to be funny.

"Let me do the smiling," she said. "You would only look phony with a smile right now."

When she was finished, she went into the kitchenette and proceeded to make a few sandwiches. Then she picked a bottle of wine from a wine rack. "You want a glass of wine or a bottle of beer?" she asked.

"I wouldn't mind a beer," he said.

She went to the fridge and took out a bottle. "Glass?"

He shook his head. "Don't need one. Just the bottle will be fine."

"Can you make it to the table?"

As an answer, he got off the chesterfield and walked slowly over to the small table in the kitchenette.

"Might as well join you," she said, filling her glass with red wine. "I like wine," she said, smiled when she saw him watching her.

"I drink it on occasion but I prefer beer." His lips hurt when he took a bite from his sandwich. Even his throat ached when he swallowed.

She studied him over the rim of her glass. He noticed that she had gray eyes, like her father. She didn't wear much makeup; her lips seemed to be naturally red. Her eyebrows looked trimmed and, remembering Morgan's bushy eyebrows, he couldn't blame her for not letting them grow wild.

"My father said to take good care of you, Lieutenant Chartrand," she said.

"I appreciate that."

"After you've eaten I'm going to examine you and make sure you don't need professional medical attention. You look a little gray. Are you

80

in great pain? Any particular area that needs to be looked at more closely?"

He tried to laugh but quit when his chest screamed at him. "My whole body is one big area of pain. Take your pick."

"I've noticed you have a gun stuck in your belt," she said. "Yours?"

He shook his head and pulled it out. "Not mine. It belonged to a guy named Steven. It would have been the gun that killed me, but I managed to kill its owner first."

"You killed a man?" Her blue eyes expressed an interest and possibly concern, but she didn't look shocked.

"It was self-defense. Had I not killed him I wouldn't be sitting here now."

"You said the man's name was Steven. How many men were there and do you know their names?"

"There were five men who ambushed us. Their leader's last name is Stiller. His father is Gerald Stiller, a lawyer. He accused me of having his brother George executed in Iraq. Then there was Cavanaugh and Steven. I'm not sure if Steven is his last or first name."

"Shouldn't be too hard to locate these guys." Her eyes were bright and large when she asked, "Is there any truth to Stiller's accusation? Did you have anything to do with his brother's death?"

Jeff returned her look. "Do you have a reason for asking me that?"

"No. Just curious."

"You know what they say about curiosity and the cat." His mouth smiled. His eyes didn't.

She didn't press. Shrugging her shoulders, she said, "It's my nature to ask questions. I'm a PI, remember?"

"So you've told me."

A strand of hair had fallen into her eyes. She brushed it away with an impatient gesture. "I didn't mean anything by asking," she said. "I'm on your side." She finished her wine. "We'd better tend to your wounds. Your cheek looks a mess. Your eye is swollen shut and even through your beard I can see your puffed-up lips. In addition to that your beard is caked with dried blood. I'm not joking when I say you're not a pretty sight."

His lips formed a smile, even though it hurt like hell.

"And please refrain from smiling," she said. "It is somewhat disturbing."

"Disturbing? I guess I assumed wrong when I thought you were attracted to my good looks."

"Let's not rush things," she said sternly, but she smirked. "Come on, let's get you cleaned up."

She walked with him to the bathroom. "Take off your clothes."

He chuckled. "I thought you didn't want to rush things?"

"Very funny. Now take them off!"

"Are you staying?"

"You won't be the first man I've seen naked," she said. "And I mean that in a professional way."

"Are you a nurse also?"

"My mother is. I used to work in a hospital in my spare time, assisting her."

He shrugged and began taking off his clothes, starting with the shirt.

"That shirt is ruined," she said. "I don't believe any amount of washing is going to get out the blood."

He agreed. The quantity of blood the shirt seemed to have soaked up, it was a wonder he had any blood left in his veins. She helped him with the shirt when she noticed how much pain it caused him trying to get his arms out of the sleeves.

Her eyes widened a little when she saw his upper torso. He didn't miss the way her tongue ran across her lips. Women usually reacted that way when they took in his physique. She touched the side of his chest and began probing it with her fingers.

"Sorry." She pulled her hand away when he let out a suppressed moan.

"It's a little tender," he said.

"You're lucky you're so muscular. It probably saved you from having every rib in your body broken. What did they use to inflict such bruises?"

"Their boots."

"They must have really hated your guts."

"That guy Stiller did. The others?" He shrugged. "They probably just enjoyed doling out pain."

"Let me look at your face."

He had avoided the mirror, but now he studied his image and what he saw did not look inspiring.

Those bastards!

"Lucky, we're not on a blind date," he joked. "I don't believe you would have invited me into your apartment." He winced when her fingers touched his cheek.

"That's a nasty cut," she observed. "You need stitches, otherwise it will leave a scar."

"Can you do it?"

She shook her head. "No, but I know someone."

"This someone is trustworthy?"

"I believe so."

"When you picked me up, I asked you if you know anything about me. Nobody must know I'm here. I want you to be clear about that."

"I know. You are wanted for murder. I've seen your face on TV and in the papers." She smiled. "Not the face you're wearing. I mean your real face without the red beard and red hair."

"Knowing who I am, you still want to help me? You're not worried?"

Looking into the mirror, he could see her studying his face.

"My father told me to pick you up, that's good enough for me. I know, I'm not supposed to ask any questions, but I'm not some innocent little wide-eyed girl, Lieutenant Chartrand. My father tried to keep his work hidden from my mother and me. I'm not talking about his work as a lawyer. My mother and I, we both know about his involvement in secret military operations."

She smiled. "I'm a very good investigator, and I took the liberty to look a little deeper into some of the cases my father gave me. Most of the stuff he gives me is simple, but some cases seemed a bit dubious to me."

"Did you tell him?"

She shook her head. "Sometimes it's best not to share with others what you know."

"Even your father?"

"Especially your father. Enough chatter. Let's get you into the shower. Without pants!"

He took off his pants and underwear and stepped into the shower stall. He would not have been surprised had she joined him.

The water felt good on his grimy skin. It stung when the spray of water hit his face. He kept the temperature just barely warm. He knew from experience that hot water on a bruised body was not the best medicine.

Jenny waited for him with a large towel and dried him off. Then she told him to sit on the toilet and let her take care of his cut face.

"Not exactly a romantic setting," he said.

"You men!" She shook her head. "Do you have to joke about everything?"

"Not everything. I think joking is our way of covering up an embarrassing situation."

"Hold still and let me disinfect these cuts." She swabbed his cheek and brow with a cotton ball, and then she applied anti-biotic cream and some adhesive bandages.

"That's all I can do." She handed him a glass and another pill. "Swallow this, and then we'll get you to bed. You need a rest."

He had to admit, that suggestion was the best thing he had heard in a long time. When he followed her into the bedroom, he noticed she had already prepared the bed.

"I have no pajamas," she said, apologizing. "You'll have to sleep nude."

He shrugged and crawled under the covers. The shower and the pill she gave him were already having an effect and he felt quite tired. He wanted to ask her where she was going to sleep, but it proved too much of an effort.

The last image he had before falling asleep was of her standing beside the bed, looking down at him with a little smile on her face.

Like an angel, he thought. A guardian angel.

* * * *

The first thing he saw when he awoke was Jenny's face close to his, studying him with her gray eyes, and he wondered if he had slept at all. Then he saw the older woman beside her. He knew immediately that this woman was Jenny's mother. He had seen her picture on Morgan's desk.

There was no denying the similarity between her and Jenny.

The same height, the same body-shape. A little heavier, maybe, and the face a bit more lined but still beautiful. The only difference was the eyes. They were a warm brown. Jenny's eyes were gray.

The older woman smiled when she saw him awake. "So you're the naked man in my daughter's bed."

He tried to grin but only managed a grimace. "And you must be the nurse who is going to sew my cheek together."

"I sure am. I'm also going to examine you for broken ribs. Jenny doesn't think you have any, but let me make sure. How much pain can you take?"

"Not much more. Why?"

"Because this will hurt a little."

She pulled back the cover to expose his upper body. Her face stayed neutral when she looked at him, but her eyes betrayed her.

He thought about Elias Morgan, her husband. He was portly, his body probably flabby with rolls of fat. What must go on in her head when she compared his body to that of her husband?

He cringed when her fingers probed his side and chest.

"It's all right," she said soothingly. "Let's see your back."

He turned around, lay on his belly. Her hand felt warm and soft on his skin as she let it glide down his back.

"Nothing is broken," she said at last. "Your ribs are just badly bruised, possibly cracked. I can't tell without an x-ray. There is not much I can do about it. Keep on taking painkillers and take shallow breaths." She chuckled. "Don't do anything that leaves you breathless for a while."

"I'll try," he said. "I trust your expertise. I can't risk going to a hospital for an x-ray."

Her face stayed expressionless. "I know."

She removed the bandages from his cheek. "I'm going to give you a local anesthetic. It will sting for only a moment. Like going to the dentist."

"I hate dentists," he said.

"Why?"

"I remember my father taking me to a dentist who didn't have a license, because he was an immigrant and couldn't practice legally. He had a little office set up in his basement, very primitive. You still had to spit into a cup to rinse your mouth. He didn't pull teeth because he couldn't give any needles, but he did fillings. Without the painkilling needle. I can still hear the drill and feel the pain when it came too close to a nerve."

She gave a little laugh. "Well, this won't be so bad then."

He felt a slight sting. After that, he was only aware of her fingers on his cheek as she sowed it together with deft fingers. When she was done, she applied another bandage.

"If you're careful it will heal without leaving too much scar tissue. Stay away from any fights, okay?"

"Don't worry, I will. Thank you Mrs. Morgan."

Looking around the room, he noticed that no light fell into the room through the window. "How long have I slept?" he asked.

"Seven hours," Jenny said. "How are you feeling?"

"Rested, but still hurting."

"I'll get you another painkiller. After that, you should get up and eat something. I hope you like Chinese?"

"I love Chinese."

Do I ever! He thought of Connie. A week had passed since he'd seen her doing that interview on TV.

"Well, I'll be leaving," Jenny's mother said. "It's getting late."

"Tell your husband thanks for the help," Jeff said.

"I will." She smiled. "He cares about your safety."

"He's a good man."

"That he is. Good night, Lieutenant Chartrand."

Jenny accompanied her mother out of the room. When she came back, she handed him a pair of pants, a shirt, and a pair of underwear.

"These clothes are not mine," he said.

"Call it a gift. I took the liberty to buy you some new clothes. I also bought a shaving kit. It's not very expensive, but it'll do."

"Why a shaving kit?"

"You should shave off your beard. My father suggests you stop running and talk to the FBI. The people who abducted you will be looking for you because you're a threat to them now. I gave my father the gun you had with you. We can probably get prints off it. You know the names of your abductors. It shouldn't be too hard to find them. I also gave him the pictures I took. We have enough evidence to prove your innocence in any crimes against the State."

Jeff shook his head. "I don't know. Let me think about it."

"Don't worry, you'll have enough time to think about your next move. You're not going anywhere for a while. Not until your face shows at least some resemblance to a human being."

Chapter Nine

Jenny slept on the couch that night, even though Jeff suggested he should be the one using the couch.

"You need the rest more than I do," she said.

He felt much better the next morning. Jenny went to work. She had a small office not far from her apartment.

"I'll be back after lunch," she told him. "I'll bring you a hamburger."

He did some sit-ups and stretching exercises just to get the blood flowing and to limber up. Then he took another painkiller for the pain in his chest. When he switched on the radio, he made it a point to listen to the news, but nothing was mentioned about anybody found dead in an abandoned building.

Jenny came home shortly after noon. As promised, she brought a hamburger and fries.

She also brought the newspaper.

"There is a small notice in the section *About Town* you might be interested in," she said.

She was right. He did find it interesting.

Thirty-seven year old Steven Mareck was found dead last night in a back lane in downtown Sacramento. He died from trauma caused by a blow to the head. A spokesman for the Sacramento Police Department says they suspect he is the victim of a robbery. Police have no suspects.

"At least now you know Steven was his first name," Jenny said.

"His friends must have found him and dropped him into that back lane to make it look like a robbery. I guess by now they know I'm still alive and, since I saw their faces and heard their names, they are aware that I can identify them. They'll be more than interested in finding me before I get a chance to go to the authorities."

"That's another reason you can't go anywhere. You are safe here in my apartment. Only my parents know where you are. And, of course, so do I."

"The wrong people might have seen you pick me up," Jeff said. "They could have written down your license plate number."

"Only a guy who has been trained the way you have would think that."

"I think of every possibility. Life has a strange way of tripping you up."

She nodded. "You need to talk to someone at the FBI."

Jeff shook his head. "Not the FBI. MacKay."

"What?"

"The agent's name is MacKay. He works for Homeland Security. His brother belonged to the same unit my brother did. He was killed under suspicious circumstances. MacKay is the man who is after me, and he's the one I should be talking to."

"I think you should," Jenny said with conviction.

Jeff still wasn't keen about that idea. "As I told you, I'd like to think about it some more."

* * * *

He spent the next two days doing nothing but rest and recuperate from the beating he received. His ribs still hurt but breathing became easier. Ugly bruises covered his body and his face showed different colors of the rainbow.

On the third day, he felt restless. The swelling on his face had gone down and his lips looked almost normal again. So did his eye.

"I'd like to talk to your father," he told Jenny at breakfast.

"I'll see if I can arrange it. He's been quite busy lately. A court case he's working on is taking up all of his time." She studied him. "Your face seems to be back to normal, except for the rainbow colors. How about shaving off that beard? It needs a trim anyway. The red color is giving way to your original hair color and if you want to keep it red, you should apply the color again. Better shave it off."

"You're right," he said, agreeing with her. "I'm tired of looking at a stranger every time I look at myself in the mirror. How about bringing me some black hair coloring so I can color my hair until it grows out naturally?"

After she had gone to work, he went into the bathroom and shaved off his red beard. Once it was off and he saw his beardless face, he found it strange to look at his former self. He had become used to seeing himself with red hair and a beard.

Maybe I should grow a beard again. Or maybe just a mustache. It made me look more...what was the word Rob had used? More sophisticated. That's it. Like a professor.

When the phone rang in the afternoon, he didn't answer it. Instead, he waited until Jenny's answering machine picked it up. It was Morgan. He left his number and told Jeff to call him.

Jeff did. Morgan answered the phone himself. "Yes?"

"This is Chartrand."

"Glad you called back. My daughter told me you want to talk with me. I'm busy today, but I'll drop by tomorrow. It's Saturday. I don't like to work on Saturday if I can help it. As I'm getting older, I'm discovering life's too precious to waste it working. Was there anything you wanted to talk to me about?"

"Yes, your daughter thinks I should turn myself in to the FBI, but I have misgivings about that. There is an agent by the name of David MacKay. He is with Homeland Security. Is there a way you could find out anything about him?"

"It won't be easy, but anything is possible. I could get in touch with someone in the Defense Department, but I'd rather not. It would be best if it were done more...er...discreetly. I just know the man who can help us there. Your friend Rob Masters."

"I thought he was still in custody?"

Morgan chuckled. "The whole team has been released. O'Connor tried so hard to pin something on them, but he was just fishing around. He had no proof. Nothing he could substantiate, anyway."

"I'm glad to hear that. Speaking of O'Connor, I may have some solid evidence that he was involved in my abduction."

Morgan didn't answer for a moment. Then he said, "Save if for tomorrow. I'll talk to Masters about MacKay."

"Thanks."

Jenny came home before six o'clock. She carried a bag filled with groceries. "We'll have shrimp and steak tonight," she announced.

"No fish?" he asked.

"Why? Don't you like steak?" She sounded disappointed.

"Of course I do, but I usually eat fish on Fridays."

"Is it because you're a strict Catholic?"

"I'm a Catholic because my parents were. Strict? No. The only reason I eat fish is because it's supposed to be healthy for you. Besides, the restaurant I used to go to for supper, served fish on Fridays. But I have no problem changing my habits. Let's have the steak."

"Good." She laughed. "I picked up a couple of nice T-bones." She inspected his face. "I like you without a beard, but I already knew what you looked like without it. Remember, I saw your mug shots on TV and in the papers. By the way, you look much more handsome in person. Those pictures weren't flattering at all."

"They never are. Well, thank you for the compliment. I worried you may not like me anymore." He chuckled. "Did you remember to bring the hair coloring?"

"I did. We'll do it right after supper."

He decided to share a bottle of wine with her instead of having a beer. Mainly because she insisted.

"I have a bottle of Merlot here that's been waiting for an occasion to be consumed," she said.

"What's the occasion?"

She shrugged. "We'll see. How do you like your steak?"

"Medium."

"So do I. That'll make it easier. Baked potato okay?"

"Sure. As long as you have sour cream and chives."

"Yes to both." She laughed. "So far we seem to like the same things. That's promising."

The steak and the shrimp tasted delicious. The wine added the extra touch to an enjoyable meal. Jenny seemed to be in a cheery and playful mood.

He helped her with the cleanup. "I don't like it when the counter is cluttered and the sink full of dishes," she told him.

Something else they had in common.

When they were done, she said, "Let's do your hair."

Before she applied the color, she took off her blouse. "I don't want to get it stained," she explained. "Better take off your shirt, too. It's the only one you have right now."

He stared at her breasts as they tried to break free from her push-up bra. Catching himself, he looked away, feeling like a teenager who just realized that the little girl he's been playing tag with has become a woman.

He knew she was aware of his eyes, but she seemed to ignore it.

When he hung his head into the sink and he felt her fingers putting the color into his hair, he asked, "Do you have a boyfriend?"

"Why?"

"Just curious."

She laughed. "Remember what you said about curiosity and the cat?"

"I remember. So…do you have a boyfriend?"

"No."

"A girlfriend?"

"Yes. In fact, more than one."

"I see. Too bad, but I guess it's none of my business."

"What isn't?" She toweled his hair dry. Their eyes met in the mirror.

"Your sexual preferences."

She burst out laughing. "You think I'm a lesbian?"

"Aren't you?"

She took a step backward. Then she put her hands behind her back and undid her bra. Released from their tight confinement, her breasts jumped free. They weren't large, but they had a nice solid shape.

"I saw you staring at them before," she said, her voice low and seductive. "You probably wondered what they looked like. Do you like what you see or are you disappointed that they are not as large as the bra makes them appear?"

He licked his lips, wondering what she expected from him. "They look fine to me," he murmured.

She came close and looked up at him. "Touch them. I know you want to."

Without thinking, he put his hand on her breast, feeling the soft but solid fleshy tissue. He became aware of her heart thumping beneath his hand. Then he felt her fingers on his belly.

"Take off your belt," she whispered. "I want to show you what I really like."

He let her undo his belt and push down his pants. When she freed his erection and curled her warm fingers around it, he let out a soft groan. Bending down, he kissed her.

She returned his kiss with great passion but kept caressing the hard flesh in her hand. When he moaned again, she took her hand away. "Let's go into the bedroom," she said breathlessly. Grabbing his hand, she pulled him out of the bathroom.

"Give me a minute," she said. "You go in and open the bed." She slipped back into the bathroom.

He pulled back the covers and lay down on the bed, his groin pulsing and his heart beating faster in anticipation. This was not something he had planned or expected. When she came into the bedroom, she was naked. He held his breath as he watched her coming closer. She was a lovely, almost unearthly vision. Like a nude goddess come down from her throne among the stars to bestow her favors onto a mortal man.

She smiled, clearly enjoying his admiration. Then she joined him on the bed and slipped into his arms. He rolled on top of her. Her legs opened and he moved between them. When he slid into her he found her more than ready as the soft, slippery walls of her love-canal closed tightly around his hard mast. A soft moan escaped her lips and she pulled up her knees in an effort to take him deeper into her. In her arms, he forgot any pain he might still have had, he forgot his problems for a short time, let her passion carry him to unexpected heights.

"Let me be on top," she said, straddling him when he lay on his back. "I've wanted to do this from the first time I saw your chest and huge biceps," she moaned as she churned above him. "I wondered if everything about you was this big."

"Are you satisfied?"

She laughed, and then she cried out as an orgasm shook her body. "Oh, yes, I am," she breathed when she calmed down again.

Afterwards, when she lay in his arms, she said, "That was really beautiful, but don't take it the wrong way. What just happened was strictly sex, the gratification of lust, which I needed badly. It meant nothing. Nothing at all."

"I understand." He was disappointed by her words but also greatly relieved. She was a beautiful woman and, as she just had proved, extremely passionate. He was attracted to her, no doubt about that, but he didn't love her. And neither did she love him. This had been nothing more than a greatly satisfying sexual encounter.

Even so, she slept in his arms that night, clearly enjoying his nearness, as he enjoyed hers.

* * * *

Morgan showed up the next day. Jenny and Jeff barely finished eating lunch, when he announced himself on the intercom.

Jenny went down to meet him and let him in.

"Is my daughter taking good care of you, Chartrand?" he asked when he walked into the apartment.

Jeff smiled, a sudden feeling of guilt plaguing him. "Yeah, she's taking good care of me," he said.

In many ways. We fucked last night and again this morning.

"Good. I was hoping she wouldn't be too much of a nuisance. She can be quite scrappy, you know, with that damn streak of independence she possesses."

"She's all right," Jeff said, laughing to cover up his uneasiness. "And not scrappy at all."

Morgan planted his bulk onto the couch. "I instructed Masters to check into that MacKay feller as you asked me to. You indicated you had some evidence against O'Connor?"

"I strongly believe he is responsible for my abduction and the subsequent murder of those three agents. I also believe Gerald Stiller, the lawyer who was at the hearing, is involved."

"What makes you think that?"

"Because his son was one of the abductors. He and his buddies meant to kill me. They never wore masks to hide their identities."

Morgan rubbed his fat chin. "Those are strong allegations. You are sure?"

"About Stiller? Yes. About O'Connor? No. But everything points in his direction."

"Do you want something to drink, Dad," Jenny broke into the conversation. "Maybe a bite to eat?"

"Just a soft drink. My stomach's been acting up lately." He gave Jeff a scrutinizing look. "I see you've shaved off your beard. If it weren't for that bandage on your face you'd look almost normal again."

"I'm feeling much better," Jeff said. "Thanks to your wife and your daughter."

"He's pretty much healed up," Jenny said, putting a glass onto the table in front of her father. "Want some chips?"

He waved her off. "No chips. My stomach, remember?"

"Oh." She looked at him. "You should go on a diet, Dad. Some exercise might do you a world of good."

Morgan laughed. "I get plenty of exercise climbing the stairs up to my office. That damned elevator is broken again."

"One day you'll drop dead of a heart attack," Jenny scolded him. "Dragging that bulk of yours up a flight of stairs is not what I'd call exercise."

"You should get married, Jenny." Morgan smiled. "Then you can criticize your husband instead of your poor old father. I'm happy with my weight." He tasted his soft drink and pulled a face. "Don't you have a regular drink? This diet stuff has no flavor."

"Oh, come on, Dad. Can I ever make you happy?" She looked at Jeff. "He's been trying to marry me off since I turned eighteen. And he constantly harps on my lifestyle."

"A woman living by herself is against nature," Morgan growled. "Especially one as attractive as you. Get married and have kids. That is the natural order, anything else is an abomination, against what nature intended. I want some grandchildren."

Jenny laughed. "Is that your problem? Grandchildren? Maybe next time I have sex with a guy I won't protect myself."

"Oh, sure, get yourself pregnant. That'll really make me happy. An unmarried woman with kids is even worse than one living alone." He scowled. "You know I don't approve of that, Jenny."

"You're a dinosaur, Dad. We're living in the twenty-first century. Things have changed. We are more open to everything, more liberated."

He sighed. "I know things have changed but not necessarily for the better. Just turn on the TV and all you see is sex and violence. Every TV show seems to have at least one homosexual in it. They are everywhere these days. In my youth homosexuality was a crime. It's not natural. The Internet is nothing but porn. Unmarried men and women have sex any time they feel like it, without any feelings between them. Young children already play violent computer games on their handheld devices. I don't call that progress."

"It's not just TV and the Internet, Dad. We're living in that kind of a world." Her eyes glanced at Jeff. "Look at Lieutenant Chartrand. He's a perfect example of the violence we have to deal with. Hell, you've been living with it all your life."

"What do you know about the world I live in?" He stared at her, suddenly wary.

Jenny poured herself a glass of wine. "More than you know, dear Dad. I know you've tried your darndest to keep me shielded from the ugly world you're dabbling in. All the cases you've given me are dealing mainly with tracking down deadbeat husbands who don't pay their alimonies and people who want to avoid paying parking tickets. At odd times you throw me a bone and let me handle a larger case, like finding a missing child."

"So? What is wrong with that? I pay you well."

"That is not the point, Dad. I want some real cases. Let me dig into Lieutenant Chartrand's problem. Let me find the men who did this to him."

"Out of the question! These men are dangerous. They are military men, trained killers. I won't put you in danger like that."

She threw up her hands. "Why don't you say it? Because I'm a girl. Isn't that it?"

He glared at her. "The truth? You want the truth? You are right. That's it. Because you're a girl. Women should not try to play men's games."

"Why not? Where does it say that?"

"Since beginning of time men were the hunters, the warriors. The women stayed in their caves and prepared the food, raised the children."

"Oh, my God, Dad. You *are* a dinosaur. I have news for you. We're not living in caves anymore. Men don't go hunting for their food. Women usually do that...in the grocery store. In case you haven't noticed, humanity has evolved."

Morgan chuckled. "How? Men still kill each other. Only instead of rocks and clubs, we use guns and bombs. If you call that evolving, yes, then we have evolved."

Jenny's voice was gentle when she spoke again. "I know you're trying to protect me, Dad, and I love you for that, because I know you care. I'm not your little girl anymore. I'm a grown woman and I know how to take care of myself. Don't shut me out any longer. Let me enter your world, no matter how ugly it may be. I can handle it."

His gray eyes studied her. "Even had you been born a boy, I would have tried to keep you out of it. The world I live in, the one Chartrand lives in, is not a world of romance and wonderful adventure. It is ugly, full of intrigue and politics. It is a world of violence and murder. It is not a place I want my children to inhabit. Especially my daughter."

"I'm already a part of it. The moment you sent me to pick up Lieutenant Chartrand, you opened the door that let me in. You've made me a target for the men who tried to kill him. They'll be looking for him and for the people he communicated with. I'm one of those people. As far as they are concerned, I know too much and I'm a threat to them. They don't know me yet, but they will find me. In order to protect myself, I need to know what I'm dealing with."

She spoke calmly, but Jeff detected the tension in her voice. He knew she was right. There was no return for her. He felt guilty for having her dragged into this.

Jenny got up and sat down beside her father. Putting an arm around him, she said softly, "I love you, Dad. You've protected me all my life, but let me grow up. I'm twenty-nine years old. Old enough to know what I'm doing." She smiled. "Just so you know, Mom and I have known for years you are not just some simple lawyer. All those trips, the calls from Washington, the military people who pretended to be civilians. You couldn't fool her. She's not a stupid woman."

"I never thought she was." He sighed and stroked her hand. "I guess I'm not as good as I thought I was at playing the role of an undercover agent. All right, I promise I won't keep secrets any longer from you and your mother, but you'll have to give me time to adjust. I hope you won't be sorry. The world you're about to enter will take away your innocence, your sense of beauty, your complacency. Maybe even your feeling of security. Once in this world, you won't be able to leave anymore."

"I'm prepared for that." She kissed him on the cheek. "Thanks, Dad. I love you."

"I love you, too, Jenny. I hope I'm not making a mistake." He rose. "I've got to go. I promised your mother I'd take her out tonight. It's our anniversary."

"Oh, right, I almost forgot. Hang on." She jumped up and ran into the bedroom. She came back and handed him an envelope. "Happy Anniversary, Dad. Give my love to Mom."

After Morgan left, Jenny poured herself another glass of wine, and then she sat on the couch and pulled up her legs. She patted the spot beside her. "Get yourself a beer and join me, Jeff. Let's celebrate. I'm part of your world now."

Jeff regarded her solemnly. Then he chuckled. "I'm not sure if that is cause for celebration. I've tried hard to escape it, but as your father said, once you're in it there is no way out of it. You may escape it for a while, but eventually it'll pull you back in."

He went to the fridge and took out a bottle of beer. Then he took the seat beside her on the couch. Lifting the bottle, he said, "Cheers."

"Cheers." She sipped her wine, her gray eyes on his face. "I'm beginning to get used to having a man around," she said. "Maybe my father is right. Getting married may not be such a bad idea."

He almost choked on his beer. "What?"

"Last night. That was nice. The sex was great and lying in your arms was comforting. In fact, I slept so peacefully, not even one nightmare plagued my dreams all night. Being married might have its merits."

"First you tell me it was just sex. Nothing to do with love. Now you want to marry me?"

She laughed, put her glass down and punched his arm. "Not you. You're too old for me."

"Too old but good enough for sex?"

"That's right. You have experience." She moved closer and pulled herself into his lap. Putting her arms around his neck, she wriggled her bottom and smiled. "Want to go at it?"

"You mean have sex now?" Her buttocks felt warm in his lap. He became aware of a gentle fluttering in his loins, felt the hardening of his penis.

She must have noticed his reaction, because she laughed and slid off him. "Not that. There is a small gym in our building. We could go and do some sparring. If you're up to it. I promise, I won't touch your face. And I won't hit you in the chest, either."

He was almost disappointed. Her nearness had awakened the desire in him to kiss her and take her to bed. "I don't have an outfit I could wear," he said.

"I have a pair of boxer shorts that are much too big on me," she said. "They should fit you."

"All right."

The gym was on the lower level of the building. There wasn't anyone else in the gym, which suited Jeff just fine. He didn't feel comfortable wearing a pair of light-green shorts made from some soft material that stretched and molded itself around him like a second skin. At least there was no danger of them sliding off.

Jenny proved to be an aggressive partner. She was a disciplined martial artist and an expert in kickboxing. With her long legs, she reminded him of Nicole. She didn't wear a gi but instead she had put on a tiny bikini. It didn't help his concentration. He had the impression she did it on purpose.

They were both sweating profusely by the time they decided to quit.

"Come and join me in the shower. You can rub my back and I'll do yours," she said, pressing her body against him.

He put his arms around her for a moment and kissed her. She laughed into his mouth and grabbed his buttocks. Then she pulled him into the shower stall. Pushing down his shorts, she touched his reacting member.

"A good workout always leaves me horny," she whispered huskily. "And this was an excellent workout."

She removed her top and bottom and put her arms around his neck.

Then she lifted her legs and wrapped them around his torso. "I hope you're not too tired," she said. When his stiff penis touched her, she laughed. "I guess not."

She sheathed him easily and used the tiled wall for support as she moved her pelvis back and forth. He cupped her buttocks to keep her from sliding down.

Afterwards, they lathered each other's bodies and let the water wash away the soap and sweat. He enjoyed rubbing her back and touching her breasts and buttocks and loved her soft hands on his body.

When they stepped out of the shower, she stood in front of him, naked and dripping water. Touching his cheek, she said, "You've got your bandage wet. We'd better change it."

Luckily, there was still nobody else around. Taking their time toweling each other dry, they laughed and acted like two teenagers after their first sexual encounter. They finally dressed and went up to the apartment.

"What do you feel like eating?" she asked while applying a clean bandage to his cheek.

He shrugged. "Too bad we can't go out. I feel like taking you out for dinner."

"There is an Italian restaurant not far from here. We could go there. Who would recognize you with your cheek all bandaged up?"

He agreed. They walked the short distance and Jeff felt elated to be outside again. Cooped up for nearly a week had left him jittery and anxious. The exercise had done him good, as had the sexual escapade with Jenny, but he needed to stretch his legs and breathe fresh air.

They ate pasta and drank a bottle of wine. By the time they arrived back in the apartment, they were both feeling good. They spent most of the night exploring each other. By morning, Jeff was exhausted, but Jenny seemed chipper and full of energy.

She got up and made breakfast while he still slept.

Then she came and woke him with a kiss. "Good morning *Sleepyhead*. You'd better get up. My mother will be here soon and it would be best if we're dressed and looking proper. She wants to pull the stitches."

Chapter Ten

"Are you sure you're the same man I saw last time?" Mrs. Morgan smiled and inspected Jeff's cheek. "You're looking so much better, even though I liked your red hair and beard." She seemed satisfied. "Your cheek is healing well and so is the cut above your eyebrow."

"It feels much better," Jeff said. "Thank you for your trouble."

"No trouble." She glanced at Jenny. "Has my daughter been behaving herself?"

"Are you asking if Jeff and I had sex?" Jenny asked, bluntly.

"Well, now that you mention it, have you?"

Jeff felt embarrassed and wondered how Jenny would answer that.

"Even if we had, Mom, it would be none of your business. I'm a grown woman."

"And very attractive, not to mention vulnerable and totally oversexed."

"Thanks, Mom, for embarrassing me in front of Jeff," Jenny said, a little flustered. "And don't give away any secrets about me, okay?"

"I wouldn't know where to start." She looked around the apartment. "You think you can fool your mother, girl. I see no evidence that someone slept on the couch. When I peeked into the bedroom, I saw the bed was rumpled and still unmade. I could practically smell the pheromones in the bedroom." Mrs. Morgan chuckled. "I don't care. Just be careful. You know how your father feels about having sex before marriage. He's still old-fashioned and I can't say his views are entirely wrong. There is too much of that going on these days."

Jenny sighed. "I already had my lecture from Dad yesterday. Please, don't preach morality to me, Mom."

"I don't. I'm not as prudish as your father." The older woman glanced at Jeff and smiled. "I can't blame you. Any woman would want to lose herself in the embrace of those strong arms. If I weren't so happily married, I might try to seduce this hunk of a man myself."

Jeff felt the heat rising into his cheeks by her bluntness. He laughed to cover up his embarrassment. "Who knows," he said, "It probably wouldn't take much for you to seduce me. It is evident where your daughter gets her good looks from."

"Well, thank you, Lieutenant Chartrand. Not only are you handsome, you're also a charmer. You know all the right words to say to a lady. I might just forget I'm a married woman."

"Mother!" Jenny said, exasperated.

"I'm only flirting a little bit with the Lieutenant. You have nothing to worry about."

"Call me Jeff. We're not in the Military here."

"Okay, Jeff. Your cheek is pretty well healed up. However, a good blow could easily lay it open again. So be careful. No horseplay."

"I'll try to stay out of trouble, Mrs. Morgan."

"Please, not Mrs. Morgan. Makes me feel old. I'm Nancy."

"Hi, Nancy."

"What was I saying? Oh, I said no horseplay. Jenny is quite a kick boxer. She likes to hit her opponents in the face. Just a friendly warning."

Jeff grinned. "You're almost too late with that warning. She already asked me to spar with her yesterday. And, yeah, you're right, she is good."

"I never touched his face," Jenny protested. "I wouldn't do that."

"Glad to hear you've finally got some sense, girl. Sometimes I think there's a man inside you because of your aggressive streak. I don't know where you got that from. Certainly not from my side of the family." Her eyes switched to Jeff. "I wanted her to become a nurse, like me, but no, she became a private investigator. Whoever heard of a female PI?"

"I'm sure she's good at her job," Jeff said. "Anytime people do what they like they usually excel."

"Thank you, Jeff." Jenny sat down beside Jeff on the couch and put an arm around his waist. "You're the first man who doesn't take offence to me being a PI, and I appreciate it." She leaned against him for a moment. Then she got up and said, "I'm going to make some sandwiches. Are you staying for lunch, Mom?"

"No. Your father and I are going for a little ride this afternoon. It's our anniversary this weekend. He promised to spend it with me."

"Happy anniversary, Mom." Jenny gave her mother a hug. "Did Dad give you the card?"

"Yes. Thanks, Darling. I can't believe it's already thirty-one years since your father and I got married. Where has the time gone? Only yesterday, you were just a little girl running around the house wearing Dad's old slippers and tripping on the thick carpet in the living room. You looked so adorable with those two front teeth much too large for your cute little face." She dubbed her eyes with a gentle gesture. "And now look at you. A grown beautiful woman. You should find yourself a good man and get married. Time is too precious to spend it alone and without someone to love and to be loved."

"Marriage is not for everyone, Mom. Many people these days prefer to stay single. Some may decide to live together without getting married. You can love someone without being married."

"I won't deny it is possible, but that doesn't make it right. The family is the foundation of a nation. When the family crumbles, the nation falls. Without families, there can be no nation. People who don't get married shuck responsibilities. They are selfish. Besides, it would be nice to have at least one grandchild."

"Oh, Mother, let's not get into that again. Just because I'm still single doesn't mean I'll never get married. People stay single longer, that's all." She smiled. "Your desire for grandchildren could easily be fixed. I don't have to be married to get knocked up."

"Hush, don't use such crude language," Nancy Morgan protested. "Don't even think about getting pregnant before you're married. A child needs a mother and father. That is the proper way."

"In your little world, Mom, and in Dad's." Jenny took a loaf of bread out of a breadbox. "I'm quite happy with my life the way it is right now. If it is my destiny to marry, I will. If not…" She shrugged. "Well, then it won't happen."

Nancy smiled. "I guess then there is still hope." She looked at her watch. "My, it's getting late! I'd better leave. Your father will wonder what happened to me. You know how he worries." She gave Jenny a quick hug and blew Jeff a kiss.

Then she was out the door.

Jenny let out a deep sigh. "Sorry about that, Jeff."

Jeff laughed. "You are lucky, Jenny. Your parents love you and they care about you. To them you will always be their little girl in pigtails."

"How do you know I had pigtails?"

"I didn't. Just guessed. You wear your hair long, probably always have. It would be only natural to braid it into pigtails. Besides, I saw a picture of you as a little girl on your dresser."

101

"Oh, you." She laughed. "And here I thought you had these great powers of observation and deduction, Sherlock."

"I have those." He grinned. "Comes with the territory."

They spent the evening making love and slept in each other's arms. Jeff awoke to find Jenny touching his genitals. When she noticed that he was awake, she laughed softly and mounted him.

After breakfast, she went to the office to check up on things.

Jeff decided to give Morgan a call. "Did Rob manage to find out something about MacKay?"

"Yes, he has. Actually, his friend in LA did. According to the files he hacked into, MacKay graduated from the Police Academy with top honors. He worked for the LAPD for a number of years. He left the LAPD as a highly decorated officer. Then he joined the DEA. He was one of the first agents the Department of Homeland Security hired after 9/11. David MacKay is an upstanding member of society, Chartrand. We couldn't dig up any dirt on him."

"I'm glad to hear that because I have decided to give myself up. I can't keep on running."

"As far as we could find out, MacKay is right now in the LA office of Homeland Security. I can set up a meeting if you want, but I'd like to be present. In fact, I'll have him come into our office here in Sacramento. Agreed?"

Jeff had no problem with that arrangement. The meeting with MacKay would be on his terms, and he would have Morgan to back him up.

"Agreed," he said. "I also want Rob Masters present. He's the one who discovered most of the information we have."

"I'll contact Homeland Security first thing tomorrow morning. It'll give you time to think it over."

Jeff put down the phone. Then he went to the fridge and took out a beer. He needed to get out and do something. This inactivity drove him crazy.

It was five o'clock when he heard Jenny at the door. "It's hot out there," she said when she came in. Then she locked the door behind her. "I've brought some potato salad. We'll have chicken tonight."

She took a couple of chicken breasts out of the fridge. "Great. I was worried they might not be unthawed." She gave him an inquiring look. "Have you ever made chicken breasts on the grill?"

He chuckled. "I'm a bachelor. I do have some cooking skills."

"Perhaps you can prepare supper while I take my shower."

"I'd be more than happy to do that."

She disappeared into the bathroom. He opened the cupboards, looking for spices. She didn't have much, but he found what he needed. Then he pounded the chicken breasts and brushed on the spices.

Jenny came out of the bathroom, naked, with just a towel on her head.

He leered at her and said, "Are you sure you want me to make supper?"

She laughed and wiggled her hips. "This is desert, lover. You'll have to wait until after supper before you can have a taste."

"Where is your grill?" he asked, chuckling.

"Under the sink. Don't grill those breasts longer than four minutes or they'll be dry. Let me put on my jeans and a shirt and I'll be there. I don't trust you."

"Now you're hurting my feelings."

"That's okay. I'd rather hurt your feelings than eat overcooked chicken." She turned and walked into the bedroom.

"You've got the cutest and most perfect buttocks I ever saw on a woman," he called after her.

"Flattery won't change my mind," she called back from the bedroom. "I need to eat first. I'm famished."

She came back out moments later, dressed in tight jeans and a red-checkered shirt. She still wore the towel on her head to cover her hair. She reminded him of Kalila. Thinking of Kalila, he wondered about her recovery. He hoped she was not facing any difficulties because of her injuries. Even though he had never seen Kalila naked, he was quite certain her body was as trim and lovely as Jenny's.

After supper, they listened to one of Jenny's CD's. She liked blues and country western.

"I don't care for most of the bands these days," she said. "I have trouble understanding the lyrics because many of the singers seem to swallow their words. I've never liked Heavy Metal or Hard Rock. Most of those guys can't sing as far as I'm concerned. All that screaming and the noise. It only gives me a headache."

"I agree," Jeff said. "I don't even care for the majority of the new generation of country singers. They have flat voices and are mostly clones of each other. Do you like Jim Reeves and Marty Robbins?"

"I love them."

"So do I. Those singers from the fifties and sixties, they had full, resonant voices. Whatever happened to them?"

"They're all dead." Jenny laughed.

"You're right. All the good singers and actors are dead." He sighed. "That is life. It changes continuously. What one generation finds beautiful, the next may reject. I'm surprised you don't care for the modern music."

"I guess it's my mother's fault. She used to play records and tapes all the time. I grew up listening to her music and I liked it," she mused. "I also like Mozart."

"So do I. It proves again, true genius is immortal. Real music and the works of the old masters will survive for centuries. I'll bet you anything, you won't hear this so-called modern music in twenty years."

"No, it will be even crazier and louder," she said, laughing. Giving him a thoughtful look, she said, "It's amazing how much you and I have in common. Better not tell my mother. She'll have us married in no time." She stretched and yawned. "I'm getting tired. Want to go to bed?"

Once they were in bed, she snuggled up to him. He kissed her gently, not wanting to rush it. When they made love, it was slow and steady. Still passionate but without the wild abandon of the first few times.

Almost like an old married couple, he thought.

Was the excitement already wearing off?

* * * *

After Jenny left for work, Jeff sat in her living room, thinking about Connie. He recalled her appearing on TV when she accused the Military of being behind Dennis Kim's death.

He had the sudden urge to give her a call. Not remembering her number, he phoned information in Fresno. When he dialed the number information gave him, her phone kept on ringing. Not even her answering machine picked it up.

That worried him. He called Detective Smith. The Sergeant at the front desk at Smith's precinct wanted to know who was calling.

Jeff told him that he was an informant and it was extremely important he spoke to Detective Smith. Nobody else would do.

The Sergeant reluctantly put him through to Smith.

"This is Jeff Chartrand," Jeff told him. "I was trying to get a hold of Connie Wu, but I can't seem to be able to reach her."

Smith didn't speak for some time, and then he said, "I'm sorry to be the one telling you this, Jeff, but Miss Wu is dead."

Jeff had trouble breathing for a second. Something inside him screamed that he must have heard wrong. "What do you mean she's dead?" His voice came out as a hoarse whisper. "What happened?"

"She was shot to death last Friday, August 3. Her funeral is tomorrow at two o'clock. It would be best if you could come to Fresno. I don't want to discuss this on the phone." Smith spoke with a monotone voice, like someone who didn't really care about what he was saying. He didn't convey any emotion.

"I'll be there tomorrow," Jeff said in the same dead tone. "Will you be in your office?"

"I'll be expecting you."

Jeff put down the phone, his mind numb. He felt suddenly dead inside and he seemed unable to formulate any clear sentences. All he could think was *Connie is dead.*

It sounded surrealistic. Maybe they had made a mistake, maybe the dead woman was someone else. However, deep down he knew he was only trying to convince himself of something he didn't want to accept as being true.

By now, her identity had been established.

His mind was in turmoil. This was the day of Michael's death all over again. This was the day he had received news of Nicole's accident and death.

Another day that would never end.

How many times would he have to go through this again? Everyone he loved met with tragedy sooner or later. How could he afford to get close to anyone? How could he justify making a woman love him, of loving her, and then losing her?

How much tragedy could anyone take and not be affected by it?

How much?

He had never been religious, not since he was a child, but now he lifted his head up and faced the sky. *Lord, is this ever going to end? How many people are still going to die until this is over?*

He sat down and put his head between his hands. Now more than ever he needed to find the people responsible. Sitting around like this would not make that happen.

Who was behind all of this? Why would they kill Connie now? That interview on TV must have made some people nervous. They shut her up the only way they knew how...by murdering her.

He didn't know why she said those things on national TV. She must have known she would call attention to her person. Why did she do it? Obviously, she had not realized the danger she put herself in.

He recalled her saying the death of Dennis and the murders of the other men had something to do with what happened in Iraq. He was inclined to believe her, but there was more involved, of that, he was also certain. His abduction and the attempt on his life were part of the whole puzzle. At first, it seemed as if Gerald Stiller, the father of the man he executed in Iraq, was one of the people behind everything, but he doubted that.

Gerald Stiller was a man who grieved over the loss of his son. He would be an easy target to let himself be pulled into something he would not normally do. As a lawyer, he knew the consequences of having someone kidnapped and murdered.

One of the people who were suspect was Colonel O'Connor.

He and his brother owned a company that manufactured arms and ammunition needed in the war in Iraq. They would be most interested in keeping the war going. By all outward appearances, they were selling illegal arms to Iraqi insurgents, possibly even to the Taliban in Afghanistan and to members of Al Queda in Iran and other countries.

O'Connor would do anything to keep from being discovered.

Mariano had been part of that group.

Galliano? He had not been a major player, only an extension of Mariano.

Mariano and Galliano were both dead. They could not have ordered Connie's murder.

Who else was there? Who was so scared to find it necessary to have an innocent woman murdered? So many questions, no answers. Now more than ever did he need to talk to MacKay. Homeland Security had resources available that gave them access to files even Rob couldn't get to.

He phoned Morgan. "Chartrand here. Have you been able to get a hold of MacKay?"

"I have. Did I rush things?"

"No, you didn't. What did he say?"

"He'll be in my office Thursday at ten. Is that all right?"

Thursday. That was in two days. He planned to drive to Fresno the next day. One day should be enough to confirm Connie was really dead, and enough time to talk to Detective Smith.

Morgan seemed to misread his silence. "Is Thursday okay, Chartrand?" he asked.

"Yes, Thursday is good. Listen, I'll be driving to Fresno tomorrow for the day. I just found out that a good friend of mine was murdered. Her funeral is tomorrow."

"I'm sorry to hear that. Maybe you want to cancel the meeting with MacKay?"

"No, we'll leave it as scheduled. I'll be back tomorrow night."

After he finished talking with Morgan, he phoned Jenny in her office. Surprised by his call, she asked if something was wrong.

"Nothing is wrong. I'm fine. How busy are you?"

"I'm fairly busy. Why do you ask?"

"I received bad news today. Somebody I cared for was murdered. I want to drive to Fresno in the morning to talk to a detective and to attend the funeral, but I don't have a car. Mine is back in the warehouse. I'd like to ask you for a favor."

"Yes?"

"I need you to drive me to the warehouse to get my car."

"I don't think that would be wise, Jeff. Someone might be watching the place. Why don't I drive with you to Fresno? I can take the day off. I'm not that busy."

He wasn't sure if that was a good idea. After all, he was going to the funeral of a woman he loved. "Are you sure you want to do that?" he asked.

"You would do the same for me, Jeff. Don't even question it."

"All right. I wouldn't ask it of you, but I'm grateful. I welcome your company."

Jenny came home early. She brought fried chicken and fries. "I didn't feel like cooking tonight," she said.

After they finished eating, she took her shower. When she came out of the bathroom, she wore a thin bathrobe. She came to him, as he sat on the couch, and leaned against him. "If you don't feel like making love tonight, I'll understand," she said, "but I'd like to make you happy." She kissed him gently.

He pulled her into his lap and kissed her back. Her nearness made him forget about Connie for a while. They made love right there on the couch. Not wild and passionate but gently and almost loving. They didn't talk, just kissed and held each other in a deep embrace. She experienced several orgasms and moaned softly with each one.

When he reached the peak of his own desire, it came with a gentle pulsing, releasing his tension to leave him at peace and without feelings of loneliness.

Afterwards, they snuggled and watched TV for a while. When he noticed her sleeping in his arms, he woke her by kissing her on the forehead. She opened her eyes, smiled and asked, "Is it time to get up already?"

"No, let's go to bed."

"Okay," she said, relieved, closing her eyes.

He carried her into the bedroom and put her under the covers. Then he lay beside her and took her back into his arms.

He was grateful for her presence. It helped him to deal with the sense of loss he felt.

Oh, Connie. I loved you and I believe you loved me too, but we didn't really know each other. It may have never worked out with us. Now we'll never know.

Jenny moaned in her sleep. He listened to her soft snoring sounds and realized he was beginning to feel more than just sexual attraction for her. Somehow, he had the impression that the feeling was mutual. Having sexual intercourse day after day and living together has a tendency to awaken feelings that didn't exist before.

What about Maxine? Where does she come in? Isn't she the one I love?

He didn't know anymore where he stood. Images of the women he had loved and still loved filled his dreams.

Nicole, Kalila, Maxine, Connie.

And now Jenny.

That's right! Jenny.

When morning came, she lay curled up beside him, a smile on her lips. A ray of light falling through a crack in the curtain played across her face for a moment. He bent over her and kissed her softly on the lips.

Her eyes fluttered open. She smiled when she saw his face above her. "Is it time to get up now?" she asked.

"It is. Slept well?"

"I feel happy." Then she became serious. "I forgot we're going to a funeral today. I shouldn't feel happy. It's not proper."

"You didn't even know her."

"You did, and that's enough for me."

"You're a terrific woman."

Her eyes studied his face. "What is her name?"

"Connie."

"That's a beautiful name. I bet she was beautiful. Did you love her?"

"When I was with her I did. She was a lovely person. Inside and outside. She didn't deserve to be murdered."

"Nobody does." Her hand moved to his cheek, stroked it. "I'll be there beside you. Let me share your pain."

Chapter Eleven

They arrived in Fresno a little before eleven. Smith was still at his precinct. He greeted Jeff with a solemn expression. Shaking Jeff's hand, he said, "Sorry about Miss Wu. I know you were fond of her."

"Yes, I was."

Smith looked at Jenny, obviously waiting for an introduction.

"This is Jenny Morgan," Jeff said. "A good friend." He didn't see the need to elaborate, but somehow he knew that the young detective suspected there was more to Jeff's and Jenny's relationship than mere friendship.

"I'm a private investigator," Jenny said. Then she added, "I'm not here on business. I'm here to lend Jeff a little support."

"It's good to have friends," Smith said. "Why don't you take a seat?" He indicated the chair on the other side of his desk. "I'll get another one for Jeff." When Jeff was seated, Smith sat down in his own chair. "You've shaved off your beard and changed your hair color," he said, giving Jeff a scrutinizing look.

"It was time," Jeff said, smiling.

"Did you have an accident?" Smith asked, still studying him.

Jeff chuckled. "Somebody tried to kill me. Luckily, the attempt failed."

"I sincerely wish they would have failed with Miss Wu," Smith said.

"So do I. What exactly happened?"

"She was shot in the park near her home."

The park near her home. Jeff knew which one he meant. He and Connie had spent a few memorable and wonderful hours in that park. Now the memory of those hours had been marred forever. "Robbery? Possibly a random shooting?" he asked, but deep down he knew already it wasn't.

"I'm afraid not. This was a planned murder. Did you see the interview Miss Wu gave a couple of weeks ago? I have a feeling she ruffled some feathers."

"Where there any witnesses? Do you have any suspects?" Jeff asked.

Smith nodded. "Yes to both. In fact, we have two people in custody."

"You are certain they are the ones?" He hoped they were, but hearing that two people had already been arrested seemed almost anti-climactic.

"We are quite certain. Vic Forester and Robert Chandler. Both from Sacramento. We arrested them leaving Fresno. We found the gun. It matched the bullets that killed Miss Wu. It's pretty much an open and shut case."

Jeff's jaw muscles were tense when he asked, "Who was the shooter?"

"Vic Forester."

"I want that son of a bitch fried!" Jeff spoke so loudly that officers on nearby desks looked in their direction.

"I understand." Smith's eyes rested on Jeff. "There is more, Jeff. On a hunch, I got in touch with your precinct in Sacramento. I talked to a Captain Stoneman and asked him about the ballistics report of the bullets that killed your brother and sister-in-law. He was reluctant at first, but when I told him about the shooting here, he gave me the information." He paused to watch Jeff's reaction.

Before he even spoke his next words, Jeff already felt an icy hand touching his brain. "What did you find?" he asked with a brittle voice.

"The bullets matched the gun we took from Forester."

Jeff sat silent, his mind numb. Even though he already knew Galliano hired an assassin to murder Michael, it still came as a shock to hear the name of the man who actually pulled the trigger.

"Vic Forster," he repeated. "Too bad I wasn't the one who found him." He felt cold inside, knowing that the man who murdered his brother and now Connie was in custody. "Who gave the order to kill Connie?" he asked.

"Dan Leighton."

"Galliano's brother-in-law? It doesn't come as a great surprise." It didn't, that was true, but who gave Leighton the order? "Has Leighton been arrested?"

"Not yet. We haven't told your people in Sacramento about him. We're still gathering information."

"Like what?"

Smith leaned forward, throwing a glance at Jenny. "I don't know your friend."

"You can talk in front of her."

"All right. I've been digging. This Leighton, he is the brother-in-law of the late Galliano, a known mobster, right? Galliano was a cousin of Mariano, the Godfather in Chicago. Remember, I gave you that information the last time you were in Fresno? Next thing I know, you're phoning me from Chicago asking me about a man named Benny Hardini, whose brother Terrence happens to work for Mariano."

"Yes?"

Smith glanced again at Jenny. "Does she know about you? I mean everything?"

"No, but go on. As I told you, she's a friend. More than only a friend," he added with a faint smile. "She deserves to know."

"Strange things happened after that. A day after I gave you the information, Hardini and Mariano end up dead. A man with a ponytail apparently shot Mariano in his office. An office that is protected by bodyguards who were expertly put out of action. Hardini got killed in a shootout on the streets in Chicago." Smith's green eyes stared at Jeff. "I find that quite coincidental. Don't you?"

"I don't have a ponytail."

"No, you don't. Did you by any chance find out anything from Mariano?"

"He gave the order to have my brother assassinated." Jeff didn't see any harm in telling Smith. He probably guessed that already and was trying to put the missing pieces together.

"Why would he do that? What did your brother do to Mariano? There has to be a connection between them. Have you any idea what?"

Jeff shrugged. "None. Mr. Mariano never got a chance to tell me. Someone shot him to death, but you already said that."

"Too bad about that. I mean about you not getting any more information."

"Yes, that was too bad."

"Mariano had a lot of friends. Influential friends. They're not happy about his demise. Some people lost money when the stocks of Banco Mariano dropped. I'm sure the rest of his activities also took a big hit. People don't like to lose money, even if it's gained by illegal means."

Jeff chuckled, his face grim. "They'll recover. The world is probably a better place without Mariano, and people should thank the man who helped him to leave this world. I won't shed a tear."

"Neither will I." Smith looked thoughtful. "You know, I've heard rumors Mariano was chumming with Senator Osborne. Apparently, he was also quite friendly with Senator Ronald Larkin."

"I didn't know that," Jeff said. "What are you implying?"

"Wasn't Larkin in the same outfit as your brother when they were in Iraq?"

"Yes. He was the CO of the outfit."

"We are trying to find out why the members of that outfit have been assassinated. Could it be that Larkin is behind it all?"

"The thought has occurred to me, but what would be the reason? He had a brilliant career in the Military, he has money, and he is a successful politician. He might even be the next president of the United States. Why would he jeopardize all that?"

Smith lifted his shoulders. "Maybe it's because of something that happened back in Iraq. Something he is trying to cover up. That's what we have to find out. I tried to dig into his personal files, but I've hit a brick wall. I don't have the necessary clearance to view them. I have no access to his mission in Iraq. The Military keeps a tight lid on that." Smith eyed Jeff. "You are a military man."

"Used to be." Jeff smiled.

Smith didn't. "You are a spook, Jeff. You can get to information a civilian can never get to. Not even a cop. I believe I've raised quite a few red flags while digging where I should not have been."

"You probably have. You should find yourself a computer nerd. Someone who can hack into government files without being detected." Jeff smiled. "I appreciate that you are trying to help me, Marvin, but as I told you before, be careful. I don't want to come to your funeral."

Smith looked at his watch. "Speaking of funerals, we'd better not dawdle any longer. I'd like to come with you to Miss Wu's funeral. How about we go for lunch? There's a place across the street."

"Sure. I think Connie would be honored to have you come to her funeral." Jeff swallowed down a lump that suddenly appeared in his throat. "Yes, I'm sure she would be. She didn't have many friends."

They had a quick lunch and then they took Smith's car to drive to the funeral chapel. The last funeral Jeff had been to was that of his brother. There had been many mourners. Michael had been a popular guy.

Jeff felt sad to see such few people in the chapel. Connie looked so beautiful and peaceful in her coffin. Jeff had the urge to bend down and kiss her lips, tell her he was sorry he had not been there to protect her. That he was sorry she had been dragged into something she hadn't even been a part of.

"Sleep in peace," he murmured, holding back tears. Now he would never know if they might have had a chance together.

When he took his seat on the bench again, he noticed a woman who looked remarkably like Connie, except she was a little taller and older. He approached her after the service. "Hi, I'm Jeff Chartrand. You must be Ashley, Connie's sister."

She nodded and gave him an inquiring look. "I saw you standing by the coffin. Did you know my sister well?"

"I was a friend."

She smiled sadly. "She didn't have many friends. Thank you for coming." She hesitated. "They say my sister was murdered. Do you know why?"

Jeff didn't know what to tell her. The less she knew the best it would be for her safety. He shook his head. "The investigation is still ongoing. I guess she was at the wrong place at the wrong time."

"The police apprehended the men who did it. They must know," she insisted.

"Like I said, it's being investigated. So far, the police department is tightlipped." He shrugged. "You know how that is."

"No, I don't," she said, stubbornly. "I've never had a sister murdered before. Right now I want to lash out and hurt someone." She burst into tears and reached for her purse to take out a tissue. "She was so young and beautiful. Her future lay still ahead of her. Now that has been taken away. It's not fair."

"It isn't," he said, trying hard to keep back his own tears. He had to suppress the urge to take her into his arms and hold her, especially since she looked so much like Connie. "I know how you feel right now," he said, gently. "My brother was murdered a few months ago. The pain will lessen believe me. It'll never go away completely, but it will get better, I promise."

"Thank you again for coming." She smiled bravely.

"If you ever feel the need to talk or need help with something, you can locate me through Detective Smith," he said on an impulse. He pointed out the detective. "You can trust him."

"I will," she said through tear-filled eyes.

Jeff walked back to Jenny, who had been watching him. "Who was that?" she asked.

"That's Ashley, Connie's sister."

"She's beautiful," Jenny said.

"Yes, she is. She's a model."

"That explains why she is so slim."

Smith came over and asked, "Are you ready to go? I should get back to the office."

"We're ready." Jeff threw one last glance at the coffin, and then he followed Smith and Jenny.

"When will you be driving back to Sacramento?" Smith asked.

"Tonight," Jeff said. "I have a meeting with a Lieutenant David MacKay from Homeland Security. I'm turning myself in, so to speak."

"Is that wise?" Smith wondered. "Could that by any chance be the reason you've dropped your disguise?"

"Partially. I have information I want to share with MacKay. Information that might possibly get him off my back. It has to do with the people who tried to kill me."

"You never told me about that."

"It's about my mission in Iraq. The brother of one of the men who was killed when we intervened in the arms deal wanted revenge."

"You just handed me another piece of the puzzle," Smith said. "Can you give me more details?"

Jeff told him as much as he thought was safe to tell Smith without putting the men on his team at risk. He also told him about Colonel O'Connor and his suspicions. He didn't mention Colonel Cowley or even Elias Morgan's involvement. Even though Smith was one of the few people he trusted completely, there were certain things he could not tell him.

"I appreciate your trust," Smith said. "What about Galliano? Has that murder charge against you been dropped?"

"No, that is still hanging over my head. I'm still wanted by the Sacramento police department for murder."

"In light of the information we've gathered from Forester and Chandler, the DA in Sacramento might take another look into the charge."

Jeff laughed. "Hardly. The DA's wife and Galliano were cousins."

"Another piece of information I didn't have. Interesting," Smith mused. "Does that mean the DA might be involved in this conspiracy?"

He threw a glance over his shoulder at Jenny in the backseat. "You didn't hear any of this, Miss Morgan."

Jenny gave a little laugh. "I'm sure there were a lot of things I wasn't supposed to hear today, Detective Smith, but being an investigator, I will have a hard time ignoring them."

Smith looked at Jeff. "Maybe we should kill her now. What do you think?"

Jeff chuckled. This remark alone made him like the young detective even more. "Jenny is all right. So is her father. His name is Elias Morgan. He's my lawyer and I'm lucky to have him on my side. Without him I'd not be sitting here now talking to you."

"I'm on your side, Jeff," Smith said.

"I know. Thanks, Marvin. Maybe someday I can repay you."

"One never knows."

* * * *

Jeff was surprised to find MacKay came alone to the meeting. He gave Jeff a curt nod when Jeff walked in.

"I believe you two know each other," Morgan said in the way of introduction.

"We sure do," MacKay said, hostility clearly in his manner and voice. He stared at Jeff. "Who killed the three agents who were supposed to bring you in? And why are you here?"

Morgan cleared his throat. "As I've told you on the phone, Agent MacKay, Lieutenant Chartrand has agreed to meet with you if you are willing to listen to what he has to say. I vouch for Lieutenant Chartrand. He is not a threat to national security. Neither is he involved in terrorist activities. Never has been and never will be. He is not an Enemy of the State. In fact, he is doing his part to protect this country from outside threats, just like you."

"Then why did he escape lawful custody?" MacKay asked.

"He did not escape," Morgan said. "Lieutenant Chartrand is engaged in military operations which I cannot discuss even with you, Agent MacKay."

"Are you forgetting I work for the Department of Homeland Security?" MacKay said sharply. "Anything that involves the security of the United States of America is my business!"

Morgan chuckled softly. "In theory, yes, but reality unfortunately says differently. You should know that, Agent MacKay. It's called politics. Sometimes one department of the government does not share files with another department."

MacKay glared. "The files I have on Lieutenant Chartrand are not complete. Everything looks perfect and in order at first glance, but there are gaps. Many gaps, especially about his time in the Military before 1991."

"There are reasons for that. Remember what I said about politics?" Morgan said.

"All right, call it politics. I go by facts. The fact his brother Michael was involved in activities with members of the Muslim community gives rise to many questions. He received money from someone in the Cayman Islands. At least that's where the account it came from is located. Lieutenant Jeff Chartrand was the co-owner of the receiving account. Michael Chartrand sent money every month to the local mosque, that's another fact. Where did that money really go?"

"I can answer most of those questions, Agent MacKay," Jeff said.

"I'm listening."

"My brother was involved in selling arms to Iraqi insurgents," Jeff said.

MacKay stared at him. "Then you are admitting he was a terrorist?"

"I didn't say that. I said he was involved in selling illegal arms. There is a difference. He was never a terrorist." Jeff spoke sharply, annoyed at MacKay's accusation and hostility. "I'm still in the process of trying to find out why. As to the two hundred dollars, which he sent every month to the mosque, there is a very simple explanation. He got an Iraqi girl pregnant while in Iraq. The money he sent helped to raise his son."

MacKay sat quietly, didn't comment.

"As you see, he didn't send money to the Al Queda," Jeff said.

"How do you know?"

"Because I rescued his son from insurgent in Iraq. Just for your information, his mother is dead. Killed by her own people."

"Let's say I believe you. Why was your name on that account?"

Jeff shrugged. "Maybe my brother wanted to make certain somebody was able to access the account in case something happened to him. Like being murdered, for instance. You should be trying to find the murderers instead of chasing shadows, Agent MacKay. But you are a bit late for that. In case you are not aware of it, my brother's murderer has been arrested."

"I didn't know that," MacKay admitted.

"There is a lot you apparently don't know. If you are willing to listen to me without prejudice, I will tell you what we have uncovered so far. You'd be wise to listen."

"Well, start talking." MacKay pulled an iPod out of his pocket. "With your permission, I will record our session. Are you okay with that?" He smiled. "I'm offering you a peace pipe here, Chartrand. I could have recorded it without your knowledge."

"I appreciate that. I'd rather you didn't record it. Much of what I'll be telling you is highly confidential and for your ears only."

"Before you begin," Morgan injected, "I think Masters should be present. He may want to fill in the gaps."

"I have no problem with that," Jeff said. "When will he be here?"

"He's here already. He's waiting in my other office." Morgan buzzed his secretary at the front desk. "Please, send in Mr. Masters."

Rob appeared a few moments later. Morgan introduced him to MacKay. Rob grinned at Jeff, and then he took the seat beside him. "Good to see you alive," he said. "We'll get those bastards."

"Am I missing something?" MacKay asked.

"It's all part of the story," Jeff said. "Just be patient."

He told MacKay about Michael and the Ten Commandos, about the SD card and Michael's journal. Then he spoke about Dennis Kim and the murders.

"As you can see, six of the ten Commandos are dead. Murdered. Only John Parker, Ronald Larkin, James Carrington, and Brian McGee are still alive. You know about your own brother and about Darrin Montana. Did you by any chance catch the interview on TV a couple of weeks ago where a young woman named Connie Wu talked about the Ten Commandos and about her conspiracy theory?"

MacKay shook his head.

"I'm surprised. Those are the news reports you should be paying attention to. She was a friend of Dennis Kim." Jeff paused. His throat seemed to give him trouble formulating the words he wanted to say. "Connie Wu was murdered last week in Fresno because of that interview. The same man who shot my brother shot her. Do you see the connection? I don't believe that was coincidence."

MacKay nodded. "I can understand why anyone would draw that conclusion."

"There is much more, MacKay. Joseph Galliano, the man I shot, ordered my brother's execution. Why? We don't know, yet. Neither did

Galliano. His orders came from his cousin Anthony Mariano, known as the Godfather of one of Chicago's mob families."

"Why would a Chicago mobster want to have your brother killed? What was your brother's connection with him?"

"None that I know of. I don't believe Mariano even knew my brother. My theory is he did somebody a favor."

"Who was that somebody?"

"I don't know. By the way, we can't ask Mariano. He's dead."

"I know. I watch TV. Sometimes."

Jeff smiled. "Good. What I'm going to tell you next involves national security, but that doesn't mean that you are entitled to hear it. I'm telling you this because I've decided to trust you. Consider it a gift. You said you couldn't find anything on me. There is a good reason. You see, I was…am, a member of Grey Ops, a Special Forces unit of Military Intelligence. I was in Iraq a couple of months ago on a covert operation. We took out a group of insurgents and prevented an illegal arms deal from taking place.

"The company that sells these arms is American Defense Manufacturing in St. Louis, Missouri. My brother took the orders for the weapons from someone who works for the Iraqi embassy in Washington. He forwarded them to a Paul Clark at ADM."

MacKay showed no expression as he studied Jeff. "I appreciate your trust. You're a spook. No wonder I couldn't find anything on you. Looks like I was wrong about you, Chartrand. Why didn't you tell me about yourself before?"

"I didn't know anything about you, MacKay, and therefore I couldn't trust you."

"You're trusting me now?"

"Yes, I am. Do you think you're the only one who investigates people? I had you investigated." Jeff smiled grimly. "In a sense, I'm in the same business you're in. Except I work for the Military." Jeff turned to Rob. "Perhaps you should fill in Agent MacKay about the mercenaries and who hires them. My throat is getting dry from talking."

He leaned back in his seat and listened to Rob telling MacKay about the Private Guards and Protection Agency in Dallas, about Nova Investments, which was owned by Mariano, and about Benny Hardini, who hired the mercenaries for ADM. "These mercenaries aren't the only ones accompanying the shipments. There are American soldiers, here and in Iraq, who are also involved."

"How do these arms get shipped to Iraq?" MacKay asked.

"We don't know yet, but we'll find out." Rob sounded confident.

"So you see, my brother's murder has nothing to do with a drug deal gone wrong, as was suggested by some people," Jeff said. "Neither did it have anything to do with money apparently owed to Galliano. There is much more involved here. We are getting closer to the truth and certain people are getting nervous. The men, who ambushed and killed your agents, abducted me and tortured me. They would have killed me had I not managed to escape. I know who they are and I will give you their names once we have established they are not in the Military any longer."

MacKay regarded Jeff for a long time. Then he said, "Thank you for your candor, Lieutenant Chartrand. In light of what you've told me, I can't see any reason why we should consider you a fugitive and an Enemy of the State any longer. I wish you would have let me record at least part of the information you conveyed to me." He smiled. "My memory isn't that good anymore."

"I've had my secretary record this meeting." Morgan smiled apologetically. "I will have her write down the key elements and the names of some of the people involved. I will fax it to you after Lieutenant Chartrand, Specialist Masters, and I go over it. I hope that will help you."

"I would greatly appreciate that. I would also be grateful if you could keep me informed of further developments." He rose from his seat and shook Jeff's hand. "My apology for doubting your integrity, Lieutenant. Unfortunately, we cannot absolve your brother of any wrongdoings. After all, he was selling illegal arms."

"That he was, but I'm still not convinced of his complete guilt. He must have had a reason for doing what he did. Michael was not a traitor to his country, I refuse to believe that."

"Well, sometimes we are disappointed by the very people we trust and love. I hope you'll find out why your brother was murdered. If only just for closure."

Chapter Twelve

When Jeff told Jenny he was well enough to move out, she asked him if he didn't like her cooking anymore.

"Your cooking is fine, Jenny." He laughed. "You've taken care of me in more ways than just cooking for me and nursing me back to health."

"Then what is it? Are you getting tired of having sex with me? Is that it?" Her gray eyes searched his face.

"Maybe that's the problem," he said, smiling. "I'm beginning to like it too much. I'm afraid where this could lead."

"What are you afraid of, Jeff?"

"I'm afraid of falling in love with you, Jenny. It may already be too late."

"Would that be so bad?"

He shrugged. "People who love me seem to have a habit of dying. I can't take that chance."

"Don't you think I should have a say in that?" She put her arms around his neck and kissed him. "Stay with me a little while longer and let's see what develops. You can't move back into your apartment because you're still a wanted man and they'll be watching your apartment. You are much safer with me."

"You have a point I can't argue." It didn't take much to convince him and that worried him a little.

She smiled and took his hand. "Come on and let's celebrate your new friendship with Agent MacKay, I know just the way to do it."

* * * *

Rob phoned the next morning at seven o'clock. "How would you like to fly to St. Louis today and visit Paul Clark?"

"Today?"

"Yes, today. It's a nice day and I feel like flying. How's that for a reason?"

"Good enough. Obviously, you know where I'm staying these days,

121

since you phoned me here. What time will you pick me up?"

"I can be there in an hour. Will that be a problem?"

Jeff looked at the alarm clock and then at Jenny, who pretended to be asleep. "It won't be a problem. I'll be ready." Putting down the phone, he bent over Jenny and kissed her. "I have to get up. I'll be flying to St. Louis."

Her arms reached up and pulled him down. "Make love to me before you get up."

"I'm beginning to believe your mother about you being oversexed," he said, chuckling.

"Don't you want to make love to me anymore?" she asked, pouting.

"Tonight, Sweetheart. Save it for tonight." He planted a kiss on her lips. "Got to get ready. I have a plane to catch."

Rob was there at exactly eight o'clock. He announced his arrival on the intercom. Jeff told him to wait downstairs by the door.

Jenny was in the bathroom. He heard her in the shower. When he entered the bathroom, he could see the outline of her nude body through the semi-transparent shower door.

"I'm leaving," he called.

She opened the door. He looked at her naked body, delectable under the spray of water.

"Changed your mind?" She smiled and stuck her head out of the opening.

"It wouldn't be hard to do," he said. He kissed her wet lips, getting some of the spraying water on his face. "But Rob is already waiting for me. See you tonight."

He took the elevator downstairs and met Rob by the door. Rob had his car parked in front of the entrance in a no-parking zone.

"Lucky they didn't tow it away," Jeff said as he slid into the passenger's side.

Rob laughed. "I like to live dangerously." He pulled into the traffic. "How does it feel shacking up with the daughter of your lawyer?" he asked.

"Who says I'm shacking it up?"

"Don't try to fool me. You're too happy this morning. If you were a girl, I'd say you're glowing."

"Oh, shut up, Rob! You're much too inquisitive."

Even though Jeff had changed his appearance, he didn't use his real name when he purchased the ticket to St. Louis for fear of being apprehended. Instead, he used his alias Dr. Callwell, the chiropractor from Canada. They boarded the plane without being questioned, but he was happy to be sitting in his seat.

When they stepped out of the airport terminal, they found it quite windy. They hailed a taxi and told the driver to take them to the American Defense Manufacturing Company.

"Is it always this wet and windy?" Rob asked.

"It's been a wet year," the driver said. "August has been mostly windy and it's time we get some dry weather."

He dropped them off near the offices of ADM. They would not be able to get into the manufacturing facilities, but the office was open to visitors.

"We would like to talk to Paul Clark," Rob told the receptionist.

"I'm sorry, that is not possible," she told them. "Mr. Clark works in building four and that is in the restricted area. Maybe someone else can help you?"

Rob made a disappointed face. "Not really, because this is not a business call. It's personal. Maybe you can give us Mr. Clark's home phone number. Then we can call him and meet with him at his convenience."

"I don't know." She hesitated. "It is company policy not to give out private numbers and addresses of our employees. I'm sorry."

"That is too bad. It would be a disappointment to Mr. Clark and to our company if we couldn't meet with him today." He leaned forward and whispered in a confidential tone. "We are agents from Jaguar Publishing in New York. I don't know if you are aware of that, but Mr. Clark has written a book, a thriller, and we are here to sign a contract with him. Perhaps you have heard of our company?"

She shrugged her shoulders in an apologetic gesture. "I'm afraid I haven't. I'm not much of a reader."

"You don't know what you're missing." Rob looked at Jeff. "Can you believe that? This lovely young lady does not read."

Jeff smiled. "That is hard to believe. An intelligent looking young woman like that."

Rob addressed the girl again. "Mr. Clark's novel will surely become a national bestseller. We're here only for today. Tomorrow we'll be flying to LA to sign on another author." He chuckled. "This publishing business is a competitive business and fast moving. You wouldn't want to be responsible if Mr. Clark misses out on what might be the greatest opportunity of his life, would you now, Miss?"

She shook her head. "Of course not."

"I didn't think so." He gave her his *hurt-puppy-look*. "So what do you say? Can you make an exception? What's the harm?"

"I'm not sure. I don't want to get into any trouble."

"Nobody will know. We won't tell Mr. Clark, unless you want us to." Rob smiled. "Who knows, he might even take you out for lunch."

She chuckled. "Not Mr. Clark."

"Why, is he an old man? Ugly?"

"Oh, no," she rolled her eyes. "He is quite handsome and not old at all. I've seen him several times at meetings, but I don't really know him that well. He's in building four and I'm, you know, here."

"Come on," Rob winked at her. "I won't tell a soul. This will be our little secret."

She laughed when she looked into his pleading face. "All right," she said. She looked at her monitor and typed on her keyboard. Then she scribbled something on a piece of paper and shoved it across the desk at Rob. "Here is his number, but, please, don't tell anyone where you got it from."

Rob put his hand over his heart. "Your secret is safe with me, I swear." He looked at the computer screen. "Do you by any chance have a picture of Mr. Clark?"

"Yes."

"Could I look at it?"

"Sure. What does it matter now?" She turned the monitor and let Rob and Jeff look at the screen.

"You are right. He is a handsome man," Rob said. He glanced at Jeff. "That will be great for promoting his book. People like to see good-looking authors."

They left the front office and walked across the well-manicured lawn.

"I guess we'll have to wait until Mr. Clark gets home. It'll be a long day. Maybe we should look for a hotel and then we'll see if we can locate his address in the phonebook. Now that we know what he looks like, we won't mistake him for someone else. There are way too many Clark's in the phonebook, but since we have his phone number it will be much easier to find him," Jeff said.

"There is a public phone booth." Rob pointed across the street. "Let's find him first and then look for a hotel."

It didn't take long to find the Clark they were looking for. He lived almost an hour's drive away from his place of work. They took another taxi to a hotel within walking distance from his residence and booked a room.

"I'll have to phone Jenny," Jeff said. "I told her I'd be home by this evening. If I don't phone she'll be worried."

Rob smirked. "You already sound like a married man, my friend. Better watch out."

"She's the one who picked me up when I was in trouble and she took care of me when I was injured. I owe her. This is just common courtesy," Jeff defended himself.

"She is an attractive woman," Rob said. "I can see how you can fall for her."

"I haven't fallen for her. Besides, she's much too independent. She's not the marrying kind."

"Well, don't say I didn't warn you. Women have a way of trapping you. They ensnare you with their innocent talk and their hot lovemaking. You relax, become complacent. Then, when you least expect it, wham! You're wearing a wedding ring. It's in their genes."

Jeff laughed. "Listen to the expert here. How many times have you been married?"

"Zero times and I'm planning to keep it that way. No woman is going to tie me down. I don't have to phone anybody and explain why I'm not coming home," Rob said with conviction.

"You just haven't found the right woman yet. You'll probably never realize it when you do and, wham! Suddenly you'll be wearing a ring through your nose. That usually happens to overconfident guys like you." Jeff chuckled. "Now, be silent, I have to make a phone call."

Jenny was disappointed when he told her he wouldn't be home until the next day. "Something came up," Jeff said.

"I hope not another woman," Jenny said with a sad sounding voice. "I was going to surprise you. Since it's Friday, I bought some Red Snapper fillets for tonight."

"Oh, now you make me feel bad. We can eat fish tomorrow night. It'll keep. Like I told you, I'm not *that* Catholic. It doesn't have to be Friday to eat fish."

"Okay, but promise me you'll make love to me the minute you come through the door. I bought a beautiful, sheer negligee. Just for you."

"I don't know what to say. I'm looking forward to peeling it off your sexy body. With my teeth." When he saw Rob's smirk he felt stupid he'd said that. What the hell! Why *had* he said that? He was beginning to behave like a lovesick teenager.

"I can't wait either." She giggled into the phone. "Hurry back, Jeff."

"I will. See you tomorrow." He hung up the phone and stared at Rob. "Not one word!" he said. "Or it'll be the last thing you'll ever say with those white even teeth of yours intact."

"I didn't say anything." Rob lifted his hands in defense. "Want to go for a drink to cool down your head? We have at least two hours to kill before Mr. Clark comes home."

* * * *

They didn't bother phoning Paul Clark since they knew where he lived. He lived in one of the smaller apartment buildings in a nice neighborhood.

The building had no security system, and they walked in without any difficulties and took the stairs to the third floor. When they knocked on the door to Clark's apartment, he opened it and regarded them with an irritated look on his face. "If you're Jehovah's witnesses I'm not interested," he said.

Rob smiled. "No, sir, we're not Jehovah's witnesses. But it is a nice day today." He pulled a wallet from the inside pocket of his jacket and flipped it open. "FBI. This is just a routine investigation and we didn't want to cause you any trouble at your place of work. That's why we decided to visit you at your home. May we come in?"

Clark hesitated. "May I have another look at that badge?"

"Certainly," Rob said, chuckling. "One can never be too careful."

Clark seemed to study the badge Rob showed him. "It looks official," he said. "Do you have other identification I could maybe see?"

"Of course I do." Rob fished his wallet out of his pocket and removed a calling card. "Here we are. There is my name. Rob Cameron. FBI agent."

"I guess it's okay," Clark said. Then he stepped aside to let them in. He pointed to the couch. "Have a seat. Sorry about the magazines all over the place." He chuckled uneasily. "When you're a bachelor you tend to clutter. No woman to clean up after you, you know."

"I know. I'm a bachelor myself," Rob said.

Jeff looked around the apartment. Except for the magazines and newspapers on the table and the chairs, it looked clean and organized enough. He could see the kitchenette and noticed a glass and a cup on the counter.

Clark wore casual pants and a shirt. This was not a man who lived a sloppy lifestyle. Jeff tried to guess the man's age and estimated him to be in his early thirties. As the girl at ADM had said, he was handsome and well built. Like someone who might have been in the Military at one time. Jeff wondered about his last name. Clark. It seemed to suggest a Caucasian, but this man had dark hair and a fairly dark complexion. He appeared to be of Arabian ancestry.

Clearing away the magazines from the easy chair, Clark sank into it and looked at them expectantly. "What can I do for you gentlemen?"

"We don't want to take away much of your time, Mr. Clark," Rob said. "Might as well come right down to business. We are investigating the selling of illegal weapons and we have reason to believe someone in your company is behind it."

That was blunt enough and Jeff was a little surprised by Rob's approach, since they hadn't actually discussed how they would handle the first encounter with Clark.

Jeff watched Clark's reaction and he had to admire the man. Either they were on a false trail and Clark was innocent or the man had the ability to hide his thoughts and facial expressions.

"Really?" Clark looked relaxed. He didn't act surprised by Rob's statement. "That's quite an assumption, Agent Cameron. I can hardly believe that. Our company has one of the best control systems in the country. We check inventory on a regular basis. All orders go through different checkpoints before they are released for shipment."

"You are one of the top controllers, are you not, Mr. Clark?" Rob asked.

"Yes, I am, and that is why I can say with almost certainty that you must have the wrong information."

Rob pulled a sheet of folded paper from his pocket and opened it. He shoved it across the low table at Clark.

Jeff knew what it was. It was a printout of an order for M-16s including rounds of ammunition. They found the order on Michael's flash drive.

"This order was sent to you via e-mail. I'll bet if we check out your computer we will still find it on your hard drive." Rob spoke casually, as if discussing something with an old friend.

Clark kept his face under control, but Jeff noticed the clenching of his jaws and the tiny tick in the man's left eyelid. He knew they were hitting a soft spot. Clark glanced at the document, and then he leaned back and crossed his legs. "I have no idea what that is. I know nothing about any orders sent to me." He stared defiantly at Rob. "You are trying to trick me." He pointed at the paper. "That is something anyone can make up. I'm not biting."

Rob chuckled. "Mr. Clark, why don't you make it easy and confess. It will only be a matter of time until you do. I promise I'll put in a good word for you if you cooperate with us."

"I am co-operating by telling you I don't know anything about illegal arms shipments from this company. I can only tell you that you've made a terrible mistake. I am a good American citizen. I served in the Military, just so you know."

"I'm glad to hear that, Mr. Clark." Rob bent forward, giving Clark a scrutinizing look. "May I ask where you originally come from?"

"I was born in Wisconsin."

"Your parents then. Where was their home before they came to America?"

Clark hesitated a moment. "I don't know what difference that makes. I'm an American."

"I appreciate that, but your parents were not born here, right?"

"If you must know, my parents came from Afghanistan."

"Thank you, Mr. Clark. Where you born *Clark* or did you change your last name?"

"My grandfather was English. That's how I got my name. Satisfied?"

"Depends. Have you been visiting your homeland lately, Mr. Clark?"

"I am in my homeland."

Rob nodded. "I guess you are. Let me rephrase the question. Have you visited Afghanistan or any of the other Middle East countries lately? Please, don't lie, because we can easily find out."

"Not that it's any of your business but, yes, I was in Afghanistan last year."

"On business?"

"No. I have no business there. I visited one of my relatives. Is that a crime?" He was beginning to become belligerent. It seemed his composure was slipping.

"No crime, Mr. Clark. Let us come back to the problem at hand. Please, don't deny your involvement in the selling of arms. We know you are the one taking and filling the orders. Maybe you have accomplices. Maybe not. If you have, do yourself a favor and give up their names. We will find them eventually."

Rob put his finger on the piece of paper on the table. "We have more. In fact, we have all of the orders for the last three years."

Clark stared at Rob. "I have nothing to say."

"As you wish." Rob stood up and walked around the table. With one swift movement, he kicked a small footstool across the room. It crashed into the kitchen counter.

"What the hell!" Clark cursed, rising halfway out of his chair.

Rob grabbed a handful of Clark's curly hair. Clark cried out and reached up to thrust Rob's hand away. Rob put his foot into Clark's chest and pushed him into his seat.

Clark cursed loudly. His eyes caught mine. "Are you going to let him do this to me?" he shouted.

I shrugged. "Yes. If he won't I will."

"This is harassment! I will file a protest with the authorities!"

Rob laughed. "We are the authorities." He pressed harder. Clark's hands grabbed Rob's foot and he clawed to push him off his chest. Rob pulled on the man's hair, making him cry out in pain. Then Rob used his other hand to punch him in the side of his head.

"Talk or I'll do some real damage," Rob said with a suddenly harsh voice. "I'm getting impatient." He pushed hard with his foot. The heavy chair tumbled backward.

Clark rolled out of the chair and lay on his side on the floor.

"Get up!" Rob said.

He watched Clark rising to his feet, and then he kicked out with his foot again, catching Clark in the chest. The man stumbled back, crashed into the door and slid to the floor. Lying on the floor, he looked up with wild eyes. Jeff saw blood coming out of his nose.

Clark wiped his nose, smearing blood over the back of his hand. It dripped onto the carpet.

"We can put an end to this," Rob said. "All you have to do is give us the information we want. How hard is that?"

"Go to hell!"

Rob casually walked up to him and grabbed his shirt. Then he pulled him to a standing position. Jeff could barely hear when Rob spoke.

"I will surely kill you, Mr. Clark. Don't look to my partner for help, because if I don't he will. You are lucky I'm the one who decided to deal with you. My partner is not so gentle."

Clark tried to shake him off. "I am an American citizen. I have rights. This is a free country. You can't just come into my home and accuse me of something and then start beating me up. I will report you to your superiors and I'll see to it that you spend the rest of your life in prison. I have friends in high places."

Rob chuckled evilly. Then he snarled, "It's funny how you people always claim your rights and scream we live in a free country. You come here and enjoy the freedom, but you will sell it all for money or for a place in an imagined higher kingdom."

He smashed Clark into the door and put his face close to the other man. "You bastard, you were privileged to be born a free man in the best country in the world, and yet, you are willing to throw it all away by becoming a traitor. If you don't like our way of life, why the fuck don't you go back to the country of your ancestors? See how you like to live in a suppressed society!"

His last words came out in a shout.

Jeff wasn't sure if Rob was acting or if he was so pissed off that he couldn't control his temper anymore. He was willing to believe it was the latter, because he felt exactly the same way.

Rob released Clark and stepped back, smoothing out his hair. He was breathing hard and he glared at Clark.

"One last chance or by God I will make my threat to kill you come true." He stood, watching the other man.

Clark seemed to have shrunk into himself. The lower half of his face was smeared with blood. His shirt showed spots of red, where his blood had dripped.

"Well?" Rob said.

"All right," Clark wiped his hand over his mouth. "I'm not going to be the fall guy. There are others involved."

"Give us names and locations and we'll see what we can do for you. I'm not a monster," Rob said.

Clark stared at him, but he kept his mouth shut. "Can I go into the bathroom and clean myself up?" he asked.

Rob nodded. "All right. I'll wait by the door."

Clark disappeared into the bathroom. Rob stood by the open door, watching him.

Jeff pulled out a sheet of paper and a pen and waited until Clark came back into the living room. He straightened his big chair and sat down. Jeff pushed the paper and the pen over to him. "Write it down."

"All right. What do you want to know first?"

"First the names of the other people involved here at ADM," Jeff told him.

Clark began writing.

"Don't write a novel," Rob said. "Just the names and what they do."

"Where do you ship the weapons from here?" Jeff asked.

"To a military base in Norfolk, Virginia. From there they are shipped overseas via a military carrier. I don't know the details."

"Write down any names you know of in Norfolk."

After watching for a while, he asked, "Where are these weapons going?"

Clark shrugged. "I don't know. Anywhere, I guess. I'm only the middleman. All I do is take the orders and fill them."

"Who are the people ordering the arms?" Rob asked.

"I have no idea. The orders come to me by e-mail and I process them."

"Who pays you?"

"I have an account in the Cayman Islands. All the money I get for being the middleman is deposited there. I don't know where it comes from and I don't care."

"One more question. What about the mercenaries AMD hired to accompany the shipments? Who looks after that?"

"I know nothing about mercenaries. I send an e-mail to a Benny Hardini in Chicago, confirming the shipment of the merchandise and the date it will be delivered."

"Okay, you've been quite helpful, Mr. Clark. You have to admit that wasn't so terribly difficult. We could have saved ourselves a lot of aggravation by co-operating right away." Rob shook his head. "I don't know why people are always so reluctant to talk."

Clark glared and put his hand on his chest. "I believe you broke some of my ribs," he said with an accusing voice.

"Take shallow breaths. It won't hurt so much," Rob suggested.

"What's going to happen now?" Clark asked.

Rob shrugged and rose. "We have the information we want. We will check it out and take it from there. If you've tried to suppress some information, you'll hear from us again." He smiled. "And the next time I won't be so gentle. Maybe I'll let my partner handle the case. He's been itching for action."

Jeff took the piece of paper, checked it, and then he put it into his pocket. He got up and gave Clark a hard look. "Like my partner said, it better be all there."

"I gave you everything I know, I swear," Clark said.

When they were outside Clark's door, Jeff let out a deep breath. Rob grinned at him. "Everyone has a breaking point," he said. "Maybe you didn't approve of the way I handled it, but you must admit, we did get results."

"We did. I guess that's all that counts. We still don't know if O'Connor is aware of the arms deals." Jeff said.

"All in good time. We'll have to gather some more information, and then we'll get a court order and have the company investigated. An audit will reveal discrepancies and eventually the guilty ones will be punished."

"I suppose you're right," Jeff said. "Let's get out of here."

Chapter Thirteen

Jenny was happy to see him when he arrived home. She greeted him with a passionate kiss and a long hug. As promised, she fried some fish filet in the evening. After supper, she went into the bedroom and came out wearing a see-through negligee. There wasn't much to it, but she looked extremely sexy and it didn't take long before Jeff made her take it off.

"We don't want to ruin it," he whispered into her ear.

"I don't really care," she breathed. "As long as it puts you into the mood."

Soon they were thrashing on the couch and then on the floor. Jeff had to admit, the negligee had done its job of turning him on.

Since it was Sunday the next day, they slept in.

"I have to phone my sister," he told Jenny at breakfast. "I haven't talked to her for a while."

Barbara had been anxious to hear from him. She invited him for supper. He didn't want to leave Jenny alone again, and he asked if it was okay to bring a friend.

"A woman?" Barbara asked.

"Yes, a woman."

Jenny didn't mind accompanying Jeff to see his sister. In fact, she was quite happy he wanted her with him, even though she told him she would have lent him her car had he wanted to go alone.

Barbara gave Jenny a friendly smile when she saw her. Then she looked at Jeff with questions in her eyes.

"This is Jenny," Jeff said, simply.

His sister nodded and studied his face. "Did you run into a brick wall or something?" she asked.

Jeff chuckled. "Not a brick wall, just some people who didn't like me. I'm fine now, thanks to Jenny."

"I'm glad to hear that. I'm surprised to see you, Jeff, since you were so worried about being spotted. Is everything okay now?"

"Not everything, but things are getting better. I'm still wanted for the murder of Galliano." He smiled. "So the less people know I'm here, the better. I don't believe your house is being watched anymore."

Barbara gave a small chuckle. "Well, that's a relief. By the way, I have a surprise for you. We have a visitor."

"Who?"

"You'll see."

When Jeff and Jenny walked into the living room, he stopped for a second and stared at the man sitting on the couch.

"Hello, Chartrand."

"Reinhart? What the hell?" Jeff looked at Barbara.

She gave him a puzzled look. "I thought you'd be thrilled."

"I'm thrilled all right! Do you know who this man is?"

"He's my friend," Helmut said from his chair. "Werner told me a little about the business he's in. I can't say I am happy, but he is my old *Schulfreund*." He glanced at Reinhart. "He is not a bad person."

"He is as bad as they come, Helmut," Jeff said. "He has no loyalties to anyone. He'd sell out his own country for a buck." He glared at Reinhart. "What are you doing here?"

"I came to talk to you."

"I don't think I want to hear what you have to say. You are lucky you are still alive," Jeff said harshly.

"Yes, I am and I feel grateful to you. That is why I am here. When you hear what I have to tell you, you will, I'm hoping, change your mind about me. I do have a conscience, you know." Reinhart spoke slowly, his German accent seemed stronger than usual.

"I doubt you do, Reinhart." Jeff had no intentions to listen to the man's stories.

Helmut got out of his chair. "I'm going to get us some *Schnapps*. Maybe it will break the ice." He looked at Jenny. "And who is this beautiful young lady? Why don't you introduce us?"

"Forgive me," Jeff said. "This is my friend Jenny. My brother-in-law Helmut." He didn't introduce Reinhart.

Reinhart rose from his seat and made a bow. "I am Werner Reinhart. I am happy to meet such a beautiful *Mädchen*. Lieutenant Chartrand has good taste."

Jenny laughed. "Thank you, Mr. Reinhart." She glanced at Jeff. "I don't know what's going on here, but it seems to me that you and Jeff are not exactly friends."

"Hah!" Jeff made a sound like a bullfrog. "That's an understatement."

Helmut came back into the room. He carried a bottle and three shot glasses. Putting them on the low table, he filled them to the rim. Then he handed one to Reinhart and gave one to Jeff. "Here, my *Schwager*, have a drink. It will make you calm." He smiled at Jenny. "Did you want a *Schnapps?*"

Jenny waved him off. "If it's what I think it is, no thank you. Maybe a mix or a glass of Sherry, if you have."

"I'll get it," Barbara said. "I'll get one for myself. Please, have a seat."

Jeff took the glass from Helmut, reluctantly, and joined Jenny on the loveseat. The drink went down as expected, burning his throat.

"*Prost,*" Helmut said. He downed his glass. "Ahh." Taking a deep breath, he said, "That puts hair on your breast."

"Chest, honey," Barbara said.

"What?"

"Never mind." Barbara smiled and looked at Jenny. "My husband is German. Sometimes he gets his words mixed up, because he translates it from his mother tongue."

Reinhart cleared his throat. "Now that we smoked a peace pipe so to speak, maybe we start palavering?"

"We're not in the Old West here, Reinhart," Jeff said, irritated. "And I'm only part Indian."

"Listen to what Werner has to say, Jeff," Helmut said quietly. "Please."

"All right. For you, Helmut."

"Thank you, Lieutenant," Reinhart said. Then he looked at Jeff. "There will be another terrorist attack on the United States of America."

Jeff sat up at Reinhart's words. "How do you know?"

"One of my friends, a German, and a mercenary like me, told me this."

"How does he know?"

"Because certain people hired him to take part in it?"

"Who? The Iraqis? Al Queda?"

Reinhart shook his head. "None of them. These people are from your own country. Americans."

Jeff stared at him. "Insurgents hiding in America, posing as American citizens?"

"No. Americans. True and blue."

"Do you have names?"

Reinhart shook his head again. "No names. My friend was hired the same way I get hired. We never know who really hires us."

"So how does your friend know his employers are Americans?"

"Because they are the same people who always hire us. I gave you the address of the company before."

"The Private Guards and Protection Agency in Dallas?"

Reinhart nodded. "That's the one. Now let me tell me you of what is planned. They want to hit the Statue of Liberty in New York on September 11. Make it some kind of anniversary. Blow it up."

"How?"

"They'll be planting plastic explosives in as many places in the lower part of the statue as is possible without being detected. Also in the ferry that brings visitors to the island."

"When are they going to do that?"

"Oh, it's already happening. It takes a long time to plant enough explosives to do damage. On September 11, one man, a seemingly fat man, will enter the base of the statue and blow himself up. It will set off a chain reaction and it will destroy the lower part, resulting in the collapse of the whole statue. At the same time another man will set off the explosives in the ferry and destroy it also." Reinhart spoke calmly as he explained the procedure to Jeff.

"Who is this fat man?" Jeff asked.

"He is not really fat. His belly will be artificial and filled full of plastic explosives."

"So all we have to do is watch out for a fat Arab boarding the ferry on September 11?" Jeff asked.

Reinhart smiled. "It is not that easy, my friend. This man is not an Arab. He is an American. He is not even a Muslim."

"Then why would he blow himself up and commit suicide?"

"Because this man has incurable cancer. He is dying anyway. His family will be taken care of."

Jeff regarded Reinhart silently. "What is your game, Reinhart?"

"My game? I don't understand."

"Why are you telling me this obviously fabricated story? Do you want money or what?"

"What I told you is true and I don't want anything from you. I'm doing this because I want no part of it. I have no problem taking money for guarding a shipment of weapons or protecting a foreign prince from being assassinated but not this." His blue eyes looked at Jeff. "I don't care if you believe me, Chartrand, but I am finished with this life. I'm going back to being a *Mechaniker*, fix airplanes. It is because of you. Because of what you did in Iraq. You are a good man."

"Who gave you all this information?"

"A friend. He thinks like me. When he heard of the true nature of his new job, he decided not to do it."

"And he is still alive?"

"Yes. He never told them of his decision. They think he is still with them, but if they find out about his betrayal he is a dead man." Reinhart sighed. "And so am I if anybody knows he talked to me."

"I don't know if I can believe you, Reinhart. This sounds just too fantastic. It is not that easy to get to Ellis Island. Visitors are screened thoroughly before boarding the ferry."

"The Statue of Liberty is not the only target. That is just a diversion," Reinhart said. "The big news is still coming. They want to assassinate the President of the United States on September 11."

Jeff could not ignore that bombshell.

"You know this how?"

"From the same friend. He is one of the three people who will be shooting the President."

"Is he going to go through with it?"

"No. But the other two shooters will." Reinhart paused for a moment, and then he said, "There is more. Not only is the President one of the targets. A number of Senators who will be running for President are also on the list."

"I think you should talk to Homeland Security, Reinhart. I cannot ignore what you've just told me." He regarded the big German with brooding eyes. "Are you willing to do that?"

Reinhart nodded. "I will."

"Good." Jeff looked at Helmut. "I think I'll have another *Schnapps*."

* * * *

Morgan's expression was grim after he listened to Jeff. "And this German, is he trustworthy?"

Jeff shrugged. "I don't know. He's a mercenary, but then again, what would he have to gain by making up such a story? I don't know about his motives. Perhaps he is a reformed man, but whatever his reasons, we can't disregard what he told me. He is willing to speak to someone at Homeland Security. Can you arrange another meeting with MacKay?"

"I can." Morgan looked thoughtful. "This is big, Chartrand. This is not something we can treat lightly. It sounds too fantastic to be ignored. It may just be true. I have only one problem with that whole story. He said these were Americans who are planning it? Why would any American want to destroy the Statue of Liberty?"

"Why would any American want to assassinate the President?" Jeff countered.

"To create chaos and unrest?" Jenny, who sat beside Jeff, suggested

"It happened before. Lincoln. Kennedy. There were attempts on Ronald Regan's life and on how many others? All of the shooters were Americans. What was their reason?" Jeff mused.

"Politics."

"That's right. It is always about politics and about power. There are rumors that the attacks on September 11, 2001 were planned by the CIA," Jeff said.

"Rumors," Morgan said. "Nobody ever had proof of that. Besides, the men who were behind it are in American prisons. They were not Americans."

"Rumors have merits. Let's face it…the invasion of Iraq was the consequence of information fed to the President by the CIA. Wrong information as it turned out. The men who came up with this wrong information…what was their motive? We are still looking for those Weapons of Mass destruction."

"Maybe we'll find them in Iran." Morgan chuckled, without humor. "Okay. I'll contact MacKay and arrange to meet here in my office again. Make sure your German friend is here, Chartrand."

"He is not my friend," Jeff said. "I hope he's not playing a game to get back at me. We'll see." He rose and looked at Jenny. "Let's go for lunch. I'm starved."

"Me too," she said.

They took the stairs down to the ground floor, since the elevators had not been fixed yet. "I guess my father is still getting his exercise," Jenny joked. "Maybe I should give the elevator company a bribe to drag out the repairs. It'll do my father good. I don't like his big stomach. It's not healthy."

Jeff held the door open for her and let her go ahead into the parking lot outside. He heard her muffled scream and then somebody stuck something hard between his ribs.

"Call out or move the wrong way and your girlfriend is dead, Chartrand," a familiar voice hissed into his ear.

"Stiller," he said, surprised and angry for being so careless. "What do you want?"

Stiller laughed. "What do you think? Now you've murdered my friend Steven. That calls for more than just a bullet in the head."

Jeff saw Jenny struggling in the grip of another man. He recognized him as Cavanaugh. He also recognized the third man as one of the men who had abducted him. He didn't know his name.

"Let her go," he said. "She has nothing to do with this whole thing."

"Are you stupid, Chartrand? She can identify us. We can't let her live." Stiller nodded to the man holding Jenny. "Take the bitch into the car. Be careful nobody sees you."

He pushed harder. Jeff's ribs were still tender and he winced when the pain washed through him. His mind raced frantically. They were safe as long as they were walking. Once in the car, he knew they'd be dead. "How did you find me?" he asked, stalling.

"I knew eventually you would come and see your lawyer. We just kept watching his office. Now move."

Jeff walked slowly in front of Stiller. They were heading for two cars parked side by side by themselves, away from the rest of the cars in the parking lot. Jenny was still struggling, trying to free herself from her captor. Jeff could not let Cavanaugh put her into the car. He might just put a bullet into her the instant she was in the backseat.

His only chance was the moment when Stiller opened the door to push Jeff inside. Preparing himself, he waited until Stiller touched the handle of the door and pulled it open. The gun digging into Jeff's ribs slipped aside for a split second. It was enough for him to react. He grabbed the door and rammed it into Stiller.

The gun in Stiller's hand went off, but the bullet buried itself in the dirt. Jeff smashed his fist into the side of Stiller's head, putting all of his strength into the blow. As Stiller slumped to the ground, Jeff's other hand reached for the gun arm and twisted it up. Grabbing the gun, he swung around, searching for the two men by the other car.

Both men stood frozen, looking into his direction. Time seemed to stand still, as Jeff aimed at the head of the man holding Jenny. There was no time to think, he let his body react to the situation.

He fired, registered the instant his bullet entered the man's forehead, saw the back of the head explode in a spray of blood. As he swung the gun over to the other man, he noted without conscious thought that Jenny, freed from her captor's grip, stumbled and fell. The other man stood exposed and unprotected. Jeff's finger was on the trigger, but he didn't shoot, hesitated. The man seemed unarmed. He couldn't shoot an unarmed man.

That hesitation proved to be a mistake. The man grabbed Jenny and pulled her by her long hair in front of him. Suddenly, he had a gun in his hand, aimed it at Jenny's head.

"I'll blow her head apart," he shouted.

"You do that and you'll be dead," Jeff said. "I wasn't going to shoot you."

"Drop the gun!" the man shouted.

Jeff threw the gun into the dirt. "Don't do anything stupid," he said.

The man laughed. "Like what? Shooting this bitch?"

Jeff nodded. "Let her go."

"No fucking way. She is my insurance. She's coming with me."

"If you harm her, I promise I'll hunt you for the rest of your miserable life until I find you," Jeff said between clenched teeth.

"Yeah, yeah." The man's laugh was ugly. "How you're going to do that if you're dead?"

Jeff had been watching him. When he saw the gun hand move, he threw himself to the ground. Frantically, his hand groped for the gun he had thrown away. He heard a shot, then another one. As his fingers curled around the handle of the gun, he hoped he could fire it before the next shot fell.

Still lying in the dirt, he looked for his assailant, but didn't see him. Then he heard the commotion, saw two figures rolling on the ground. He rose quickly, rushed forward, gun in hand.

The two figures separated. It was Jenny who rose, crouched over her opponent. The man on the ground shouted hoarsely as she smashed her foot into his face.

"Nobody puts a gun to my head, you son of a bitch!" Jenny yelled. "Nobody!"

She kicked the man one more time. He was lucky she wore sneakers instead of high heels. Blood spurted from his ruined nose.

Nancy Morgan's warning popped into his head. *She likes to hit her opponent in the face.*

Jenny stood over her would-be abductor like an angel of death. Her black hair looked disheveled and her face was pulled into an angry mask. Jeff found her terribly attractive in her fury.

He walked up to her and pulled her away. "We'll have to leave," he said, gently.

"And let this bastard live?" she hissed.

"The police will deal with him. He's not going anywhere."

"Let's make sure of that," she said. "Give me the keys," she said to the man groveling on the ground. Moaning, he searched in his pocket and pulled out his car keys. Jenny put them into one of her jean pockets. "*Now* you're not going anywhere."

She looked at Cavanaugh lying motionless beside the car. Blood soaked from his destroyed head. "I guess he's dead," she said.

Jeff nodded. He walked around the second car and searched for Stiller. He lay unconscious from the blow to his head. "We'd better get his keys also," he said.

Jenny went through Stiller's pockets and found them. She pocketed them. "We'll go back to my father's office," she said.

Jeff agreed. He wiped Stiller's gun carefully with his shirt and put it into the man's hand. "Let the police try to figure out what exactly went down here."

"Are those the men who abducted you?" Jenny asked as they ran back into the building.

"Yes."

"You should have killed those other two. They deserved it."

"It would have been murder."

"I thought you were what they call a *spook*?" Jenny asked. "Aren't you supposed to be this cold assassin without a conscience?"

He gave her a sidelong glance. "Is that what you think of me? A cold heartless assassin?"

"I don't know what to think," she said. "I watched you as you shot the man who held me. Your eyes, they were like ice, just like your face. The face of death, that's the only way I can describe it." She gave a little shudder. "I hope I never have to look into those eyes again."

They had reached the top of the stairs and rushed toward Morgan's office. He was surprised to see them. He looked at Jenny. "My God, what happened? You look as if someone dragged you through a barrel of dirt."

"Call the cops, Dad," Jenny said. "There has been a shooting."

* * * *

They met with MacKay the next day. When Jeff told him about the shooting, he said, "You have a talent for getting into trouble, Chartrand. Why didn't you talk to the local police?"

Jeff smiled grimly. "I'm still wanted for murder in the Galliano case. Now I was involved in another shootout. How good does that look, MacKay?"

"I can see your problem." MacKay looked troubled. "You can't keep running, Chartrand. Eventually you will have to turn yourself in. I don't feel comfortable with this whole situation. I don't want to be dragged into your affairs as an accomplice or some other charge. As you pointed out the first time we met, I may be Homeland Security, but I also am bound by the laws of this country. Even I can't get away with murder."

"I didn't murder anyone," Jeff said. "I admit, I've shot people, but they deserved to die. It was done as part of my job. Galliano was one of them. I shot him in self-defense."

You shot Mariano in cold blood, his conscience screamed.

In cold blood, yes, but he went for his gun.

He was unarmed when you shot him.

He deserved to die!

Jeff looked at MacKay. "These were the men who abducted me, MacKay. They came back to finish the job. The one I shot would have shot Miss Morgan the moment she was inside his car. I had no choice but to shoot him. I didn't shoot the other two even though I could have. They would have had no such compunction. They would have killed me without mercy. Think about that."

MacKay shrugged. "I'm not going to judge you, Chartrand. I believe you. Now…what is this thing about a conspiracy involving September 11?"

"We're waiting for the man who will tell you all about it," Morgan said.

He barely finished speaking when Morgan's secretary knocked on the door. "Mr. Reinhart is here," she announced.

The big German walked into the room and nodded to Jeff.

"This is Agent MacKay from Homeland Security," Jeff said. "He is the man who will be your best friend after you tell him everything you've told me, *Herr* Reinhart."

Reinhart shook MacKay's hand and took a seat across from him. "I hope you have a good memory," he said, "because I have much to tell you."

"I don't," MacKay said, smiling. "I rely on this." He pointed to a small electronic recorder on the table. "It is much more reliable than my memory."

Jeff stayed in the room when Reinhart told his story to MacKay. The Agent listened very carefully and with great interest. He never interrupted Reinhart until the German stopped talking. Then he fired question after question at him, possibly hoping to trip him up, but Reinhart stuck to everything he had said.

"You're sure all the dates and locations you gave me are correct?" MacKay asked.

Reinhart chuckled. "I have a near perfect photographic memory. I don't forget dates and places. People's faces I don't forget either. I have some trouble with names, sometimes, but most of the time I even remember all of them. In this case, I remember everything. Trust me."

"Well, Mr. Reinhart, I thank you for this information. We will certainly investigate what you've told me."

"Take my advice, Agent MacKay, don't spend too much time investigating. Act before it is too late. If the things I told you about do happen, it will be a bad time for America. Possibly for the world. Don't let it happen, okay?"

"I won't. Thank you again."

Chapter Fourteen

Jeff looked up at the partially visible moon in the night sky, and then at the cottages hidden among the trees. The training camp of the terrorists lay silent, but he knew they had sentries watching for possible intruders.

According to Reinhart's information, there should be about twenty-five men sleeping inside the three cottages. When Jeff looked through his night glasses, he could see one of the guards sitting in the shadows on the porch of the first cottage. His M-16 leaned against the wood siding within easy reach.

Jeff didn't think the guards would be too alert because they didn't expect anyone showing up in this secluded spot. A fact that should be in the invading team's favor.

At first, MacKay had been reluctant to let Jeff take part in the operation, but then Jeff convinced him he could be a valuable member of the squad.

After trudging for three hours through nearly impenetrable territory, he questioned his decision to be here. Even though he had sprayed his face and hands with insect repellant, the mosquitoes seemed to find areas he'd forgotten. Or maybe they just ignored the sprayed parts of his skin.

The camp was located in the great wilderness area of Montana, beside one of the many lakes. There were no roads or trails to follow. Even if there had been, they could not have come near the camp with motorized vehicles. The only one way to get to the camp without being spotted was to walk.

The cottages he looked at were primitive, built from local materials. They reminded Jeff of pioneer homes he had seen in pictures of the early settlers. This was a perfect hideout for people involved in illegal activities.

There were three cottages, which meant three sentries. Possibly one more away from the buildings, but Jeff doubted that.

He saw one of MacKay's men crawling toward the first cottage.

Two more men were targeting the other two buildings. The three guards would be taken out simultaneously.

The man on the ground rose silently, used the side of the cottage to keep hidden. Then he stepped onto the porch. The guard must have heard or sensed something, because he lifted his head, turned it in the direction of his approaching assailant. He tried to grab his M-16, but he was too late. His attacker reached him before he even touched his weapon. A short scuffle, and then the guard slid to the ground, limp and unmoving.

"Phase two," came MacKay's order over the comm. Jeff rose and moved through the trees toward the cottage. He saw the other members of the team doing the same. Some headed for the first cottage, the rest for the other two buildings.

Jeff had crossed about half the distance, when he saw the beam of a flashlight suddenly among the trees. He heard a shout, then the sound of a gunshot.

"Son of a bitch!" someone cursed in Jeff's comm.

"What the hell happened?" MacKay sounded irritated.

"This guy must have been in the outhouse."

Jeff ran toward the cottage. He saw dim light through the small window. Then the door opened and a man carrying a submachine gun stepped out. The agent on the porch pulled him outside. Another man appeared in the door. When he saw the two struggling men, he shouted.

One of the approaching agents opened fire. The man fell. Jeff reached the cottage, heard the breaking of glass, saw the barrel of a rifle in the window. He was close, reached up and pulled hard. The rifle went off, but then it was ripped from his grip.

More agents jumped onto the porch. One of them threw a smoke bomb through the door into the cabin.

Shots rang out from the other cottages. Men screamed. Two men appeared in the doorway, cursing and shouting. The staccato of their M-16s echoed through the trees, and then they fell in the hail of bullets that cut them down.

Suddenly it was silent.

Jeff heard men coughing inside the cottage. Then someone shouted. "Don't shoot. We're coming out." Coughing, their empty hands up, a number of men dressed only in shorts and tee shirts stumbled out. MacKay's men surrounded the terrorists, handcuffed them and herded them away from the cottages.

"Check out each building," MacKay ordered a few of the agents.

"Make sure no one is hiding inside. Be careful."

The picked agents donned gasmasks and entered the cottages, their weapons ready. A couple of the other agents set up a number of battery-operated floodlights. Jeff looked over the assembled terrorists. He didn't see anyone who could be described as Arabic looking.

"May I ask what this is all about?" one of the captives asked.

MacKay walked up to him. "You are hereby charged with planning a terrorist attack on the United States of America. Satisfied?"

"What are you talking about? We are no terrorists. We're just a group of hunters and survivalists."

"Hunters with M-16s? Who are you kidding?"

"We're training for an eventual attack on the United States by hostile forces."

"Really? Well, you can explain all of that to a judge. Until then consider yourself under arrest."

"This is a mistake," the man protested. "You've murdered some of my friends."

"They came at us firing their weapons. We returned fire in defense."

The man laughed. "In defense? You attacked us in the middle of the night. What were we to assume? It is us who did the defending."

"Save your arguments for your court case. Now shut up! Anyone else wants to protest?"

One of the men lifted his hand. "Can I talk to you in private, sir?"

Jeff noticed his heavy accent and guessed who the man might be. MacKay must have had the same thought. He looked at Jeff and said, "You talk to him, Lieutenant."

"Yes, sir," Jeff said. Then he told the man to come with him.

When they were out of earshot from the others, the man said, "My name is Herman Klauss. I'm asking for protection. If the others find out what I did I'm a dead man."

"I know who you are," Jeff said. "Your friend Werner Reinhart told me about you."

"You know Werner?"

"Yes. We are acquaintances. I'll grant you protection, but it would be best if none of your friends suspects anything right now. I'll walk with you to the outhouse and I'll tell them you had an attack of the runs. Okay?"

"Okay. Thank you."

The outhouse was some distance from the cabins. Klauss went

inside and Jeff waited for him until he came back out. Then he accompanied the man back to the rest of the assembled prisoners.

"He had to take a crap," Jeff said, laughing. "Some scary terrorist, hey?"

A few of the agents joined his laughter. The men who had been checking out the cabins came back out. "All clear," one of them said.

"All right, let's move out!" MacKay barked.

He must have turned off his comm., because Jeff couldn't hear what he said into his cell phone, but he didn't have to hear it. He knew MacKay gave orders to the men who were on standby at the mouth of the river that spilled into the lake on the far end.

Moments later he heard the rumble of heavy engines as the three motorboats came racing across the lake to pick them up. Jeff shouldered his M-16 and followed the squad and the prisoners down to the lakeshore. He saw a couple of large boats moored nearby. If the terrorists had been smarter, they would have had guards stationed on at least one of the boats, in case someone decided to drop in for a visit from the lake.

When the three boats arrived, they floated about fifty feet away from shore because of the depth of the water. The prisoners had to enter the water and walk the distance to the boats.

The boats were not large and the prisoners squeezed together into the available space. Each of the boats would have only a couple of armed agents on board to guard the prisoners. The rest of the team boarded the two boats of the terrorists and one of those boats took the lead, while the others followed.

Jeff was in the last boat, which also carried the dead. He had counted seven lifeless bodies, all of them terrorists. None of the agents had been injured or died, which was a relief.

As the loaded boats glided across the water, he noticed that the sky was getting lighter. The sun would be coming up soon.

The trip down the river was rough, with many boulders blocking the way, but they arrived safely at the rendezvous spot where four army trucks were waiting for them to pick them up.

When Jeff finally sat in the back of one of the trucks, he relaxed. He felt tired, his mosquito-bitten face and neck itchy, but he was satisfied. The operation had been successful, the terrorist attack prevented. He knew that agents were already checking out Ellis Island, the ferry, and the Statue of Liberty for hidden explosives.

September 11 would be coming and going without loss of life or property. The President would survive and so would the men who wanted his job.

For Jeff this was just another violent day in a series of violent days. The majority of American people would be waking up right now and go about their daily activities, enjoying their freedom and feeling safe, without giving much thought to the men who risked their lives every day to guarantee that freedom.

Freedom! Freedom of speech and human rights for everyone. What a wonderful concept! To be able to do what you wanted. To be able to travel without fear for your safety and to go to bed each night without worrying about the next day. Everybody who had this freedom took it for granted. The ones who didn't have it wanted to take it away from the ones who did.

And then there were people like the ones they just apprehended. People without conscience, who sold out their country for money and for power. Who didn't give a crap about the lives or rights of anyone or the damage they inflicted.

We should have lined them up and shot them down like rabid dogs.

That would, of course, have been barbaric and murder and would have violated their civic rights. The very laws they wanted to destroy protected them. What irony!

Jeff closed his eyes and thought about his brother Michael, about Connie and all the other people who had lost their lives defending their right to be alive and to live in this country.

* * * *

"I thought you might be interested in what we found out from the prisoners." MacKay's attitude toward Jeff had changed since the raid on the terrorist camp. He seemed more amiable and almost acted like a good friend.

"I am," Jeff said.

"I can be in Sacramento tomorrow. We could meet again in Morgan's office. I would prefer if he were also present." He paused. "Some of the information might be connected to your brother Michael."

"I understand. Thank you for calling, Agent MacKay. I'll see you tomorrow."

Jeff put down the phone and looked at Jenny. "I'll have to meet MacKay at your father's office tomorrow morning. Can you drive me?"

"Of course. If you don't mind, I'd be interested in what he found out."

"I'm sure that can be arranged."

She touched his cheek and ran her fingers along his jaw. "You look almost normal again. My mother did a good job sewing you up."

"She did and I'm grateful." He pulled her close and kissed her. "I'm grateful for a lot of things. To your mother and to you for taking such good care of me in many ways." He chuckled. "Still are."

"That is because I love you, Jeff."

"I know. I love you too."

Over a week had passed since Stiller and his men attacked them. If there were any witnesses to that incident, no one came forward. The police took Stiller and the other man into custody. So far, they had not implicated Jeff or Jenny, and Jeff didn't think they would.

As far as the police were concerned, the three men were victims not aggressors. Stiller and his surviving companion would go free unless the police implicated Stiller in shooting one of his friends, since he was found with the gun in his hand. Stiller would have some explaining to do, but Jeff didn't think he'd have trouble convincing the police of his innocence. Especially with a lawyer as a father.

Jeff didn't have any doubts though that he and Jenny were still in danger. Stiller would try again. They would have to be on guard at all times. Neither of them would be safe until they were dead or until Stiller was taken care of. He didn't want to think about that now, but he wasn't going to relax either.

The next morning, he read the newspaper before breakfast but still didn't find anything that might hint on the mission in the Montana wilderness, which was a good sign. He and Jenny finished breakfast, and then they drove to Morgan's office.

MacKay wasn't there yet but Rob was.

"I thought I'd invite Masters to the meeting," Morgan said. "I have a feeling this whole thing isn't over yet."

MacKay arrived a few minutes later. He came right down to business. "As you can imagine, most of those guys insisted they were just a bunch of survival nuts, but a couple of them finally confessed."

"What about Herman Klauss, the man who informed us of this plot?" Jeff asked.

"He is still in custody, in protective custody, until we've sorted out everything. We promised him amnesty and a free trip back home to Germany. He agreed to the terms." MacKay's eyes were solemn when he carried on, "One name came up that will be of great interest to you,

Chartrand. Apparently, he is the man behind this whole thing. John Parker. "

"John Parker?" Jeff repeated. "That is hard to swallow. He is a decorated war hero. Why would he be planning a terrorist attack on his own country or try to have the President assassinated?"

"Why indeed. I'm not going into details about the planned attack, the short version will be sufficient. As you know, John Parker is the bodyguard and good friend of Senator Ronald Larkin."

"Does that mean that Larkin is also involved?"

"He might be, but we don't believe he is one of the string pullers. We've arrested Parker. He denied everything until yesterday morning. He claims he is just another puppet and asked to make a deal if he gives us the names of the people who are really behind it."

"Did he tell you why they wanted to do this?"

"Oh, yes, and it is indeed a devilish and sinister plot. The destruction of the Statue of Liberty and the assassination of our President would be blamed on Al Queda, the Taliban, Iran, or some other Islamic group or country. The American people would be outraged and cry revenge. Of course, the media, who is controlled by people who are involved in this plot, would fuel the anger. It would give the new administration a reason to invade any country that has shown aggression toward the United States of America, like Iran for instance. It's been in the books for a long time and it wouldn't take much to convince the Military. Some of our top generals are itching for an opportunity to start another mission. The next on the list would be Pakistan for allowing the Taliban to use that country to hide and regroup."

"Why assassinate the President?"

"It would allow certain groups to put a puppet into the Whitehouse."

"Who's the puppet?"

"Ronald Larkin."

"How can anyone be sure he will be elected?"

"By getting rid of all the other candidates, including the Vice President."

"Wow!" Jeff blew air across his lip. His eyes were grave. "Don't keep us in suspense. Who are these people behind all of this?"

"Anthony Mariano was one of them. Of course, he is dead now. The others are Senator Kenneth Osborne, Colonel O'Connor and his brother Harry O'Connor. The CEO of United Oil Conglomerate, Herman Weinberg, is another one. The list is by no means complete. There are others."

"Did Parker give you a reason why they would want to commit such a horrible act?" Jenny asked.

"Power and money. All of these men are in the oil business. They want control over the oil in the Middle East."

Rob cleared his throat. "If I may, these confessions coincide with my findings. All the men on your list have large shares in United Oil Conglomerate. UOC controls a great number of oil refineries and oil producing smaller companies. UOC also owns shares in American Defense Manufacturing, of which Colonel O'Connor and his brother are the largest shareholders. We already know that ADM is selling illegal arms to insurgents. John Parker is a shareholder in that company, as is his father, retired General Mathew John Parker, who, incidentally, also owns shares in UOC. In other words, John Parker is not the innocent puppet he claims to be. He is in on the whole thing."

"One happy family," Jeff commented.

Rob nodded. "As you may know, Senator Osborne has already publicly announced his agenda. In his words, *We appreciate what the Canadians are doing in Afghanistan, but it is not enough. The Taliban are gaining power again. The US needs to have a stronger presence in Afghanistan.* He made his thoughts quite clear when he said we need to get control over the whole region. According to Senator Osborne, the United States of America needs to control the world's oil supply."

Jeff chuckled. "By that he means the American oil companies need to control the flow of oil."

"That is precisely what he means."

"Those bastards," Jenny said with conviction. "I hope you are going to arrest them."

"If Specialist Masters can substantiate his findings and with what we got from the men we have in custody, I believe we have a good case," MacKay said.

"We'll need a court order to have both of those companies investigated," Rob said. "I'd be willing to bet we'll find plenty evidence at American Defense Manufacturing." Rob glanced at Jeff. "Something else I discovered. The maiden name of John Parker's wife used to be Mariano."

"She is related to Mariano?" Jeff asked, surprised by the revelation.

"You can say that. She is his daughter." Rob let that bombshell sink in, waited for Jeff's reaction.

Jeff stared. "Are you sure about that?"

"Oh, yes." Rob chuckled. "There is the connection we were looking for between Parker and the Godfather. By the way, his father, General Parker, has shares in Banco Mariano, which, incidentally, has branches in Mexico, Italy, Brazil and, yes, in the Cayman Islands."

"That is also quite revealing. Some things are beginning to make sense, for instance it is clear now who transferred money to certain accounts," Jeff said.

"Right. That and who collected the payments for the weapon's orders, and who paid American Defense Manufacturing. The fact Banco Mariano has shares in ADM speaks volumes."

"I don't quite follow your conversation," MacKay said.

"Masters and I took the liberty to talk to an employee of ADM," Jeff said. "We persuaded him to confess that he is involved in the selling of illegal arms." He hesitated for a moment. "My brother Michael kept good records of all the transactions."

"We checked your brother's hard drive," MacKay said. "There was nothing on it."

Jeff smiled. "We have a flash drive. We will make it available to you for inspection."

"Does this mean your brother was involved in the dealing of illegal weapons?"

Jeff nodded. "From what I discovered, yes, he was. I don't know why."

"There is still some stuff we haven't looked at," Morgan said. "Remember the envelope you gave me for safekeeping, Chartrand?"

"The one Brian McGee left with Connie Wu? I remember."

"In light of recent developments and Miss Wu's demise, I'd say we can safely open that envelope and have a look at its contents. We didn't make any promises to McGee."

"I see no harm in it, "Jeff said. "It may contain answers to our questions."

"I have it locked away in my safe," Morgan said. He left the room to get the envelope.

Jeff was anxious and a little apprehensive of what they might discover. The revelation that John Parker's wife was the daughter of the late Anthony Mariano implied a terrible truth.

Chapter Fifteen

Morgan came back into the room, slit open the large manila envelope with a letter opener.

When he put the opener back onto the desk, Jeff noticed that the handle was made from transparent plastic. Inside the handle, he saw a picture with palm trees and a beach.

For some reason that seemed to have some significance. Jeff stared at it and his thoughts began to wander for an insane moment. To be lying on that beach right now, under the palm trees, watching the waves rush to the sandy shore, to hear the surf, to go swimming in the ocean.

He realized he needed a change in scenery. He needed to get away from all this violence, before it overwhelmed him.

He watched Morgan empty the contents of the envelope onto the shiny surface of the desk.

A few sheets of paper and a flash drive.

Morgan picked up a couple of sheets. He handed them to Jenny. "Do us the honor and read it, Jenny."

She looked at the sheet and began reading.

* * * *

To whom it may concern:

My name is Brian McGee. I swear that the following account of events is the absolute truth.

From April 2003 until July 2004, I was in Iraq. I was a member of a military unit we called the Ten Commandos. Our unit consisted of ten soldiers. The other member of our unit were

Captain Ronald Larkin. He was our CO.

Staff Sergeant John Parker.

Lieutenant John Mackay. He was the medic of our unit.

Lieutenant Michael Chartrand.

Corporal Toby Miller.

Corporal Ethan Grey.

Private Dennis Kim.

Private James Carrington.

Corporal Darrin Montana.

On the night of January 8, 2004, something terrible happened. I have carried this secret with me since the incident and it has been eating at my soul.

We had just returned from a mission and we decided to celebrate, since it was Captain Larkin's birthday. Most of us got pretty drunk, except for Sergeant Parker. He didn't drink, but he encouraged Captain Larkin to drink more than he should have.

The Sergeant promised Captain Larkin a special birthday present. When the Captain was so drunk that he didn't know anymore what he was doing, Sergeant Parker brought in the present.

An Iraqi girl. She was very pretty and extremely young. It was obvious to us she didn't want to be here.

When the Sergeant told her to lie down on the floor, she refused. He hit her. Then he ripped off her clothing until she was naked. He pinned her to the ground and urged Captain Larkin to have sex with her. He said he paid her a lot of money and this was what she wanted. It was all right. This was just a game to make it more exciting.

We didn't believe him, but Captain Larkin was too drunk to think clearly. So he raped the girl. I can still hear her screams in my nightmares.

After the Captain finished with her, Sergeant John Parker shot her in the head. He murdered her in cold blood.

Michael got it all on his digital camera.

It all happened so fast we could do nothing. Parker threatened to kill us if we told anybody about it. He said we were all guilty by association anyway and it would be best if we all kept our mouths shut. Forever.

It wasn't hard to intimidate us. All of us were guilty of more than just one crime.

Somehow, Parker talked us into taking part in selling weapons to Iraqi militants. It was no big deal, he said, because the weapons we sold were antiques, worth nothing to the Military, but we could be making a lot of money.

Then there was the incident with the hospital, when we killed innocent civilians because somebody gave us the wrong information.

No, none of us was innocent, but raping and killing an innocent girl was not something we wanted to be part of.

But we were.

John Parker shot John MacKay two days after MacKay told everybody he would not be intimidated. He was going to report the incident. Parker shot him in the back during a short engagement with an Iraqi group of insurgents. Parker said it was an accident. Friendly fire.

A week later, Parker shot and killed Darrin Montana, who had also indicated he would go and make a report. There were no witnesses to the shooting, but we are certain Sergeant Parker shot Darrin. It happened when they went on patrol to investigate rumors of insurgents planting roadside bombs. When they returned, Darrin Montana was dead. Parker claimed insurgents killed him. None of us believed it but we did nothing.

John Parker has blackmailed us ever since. He forced us to take part in selling illegal weapons to insurgents, even after we were discharged from the army. He threatened to personally kill us if any of us ever talked or if we tried to leave the group.

Once a member of the Ten Commandos, always a member.

Until death do us part!

Michael Chartrand and Dennis Kim agreed to work with Parker and handle the transactions if he left the others alone.

Neither of them ever felt right doing it, but they had no choice. Only when orders came in for helicopters and tanks, Michael refused to go along with it.

That's when Parker fulfilled his promise.

Michael Chartrand was the first. Then came Toby Miller and then Dennis Kim. Ethan Grey went crazy, he ended up in an asylum, but in the end they got to him also.

Now James Carrington and I are the only survivors, aside from Captain Larkin, but John Parker won't kill him, because he has him in his pocket. After Larkin becomes President, John Parker will be one of the most powerful men in America.

I am afraid for my life. When you read this, I am probably dead.

Don't let our deaths go unpunished.

June 28, 2007

Brian McGee

* * * *

"Is this McGee dead?" MacKay asked.

Jeff noticed that his face was tight, and his eyes cold and empty. "Not as far as I know," he said.

"We'll have to find the man. I need to talk to him. His testimony will put Parker away, maybe even send him to the chair," MacKay said, his jaws working.

"There are more pages here," Morgan said, handing them to Jenny.

"These are handwritten," she said. "They look like pages from a journal."

"May I see them?" Jeff asked.

When he looked, he saw that his assumption had been correct. "They are the missing pages from my brother's journal." He gave them back to Jenny. "You read them. I don't think my throat will obey me."

Jenny began reading. It was more or less a slightly different version of what McGee had written.

"...It was terrible. We shot and killed innocent civilians. According to Intelligence reports, there should have been Iraqi soldiers hiding in that hospital. But the information proved wrong. There were no soldiers. Only civilians. Old men, women and children..."

Jenny looked up. She seemed to have trouble with her eyes. She blinked a few times. Her voice sounded somewhat hoarse when she continued. When she came to the part where Michael described the rape and murder of the Iraqi girl, she stopped again and wiped her eyes.

"I don't know if I can go on reading," she said with a teary voice. "This is just so awful."

Jeff took the sheets of paper from her hands and scanned them. "He's talking about the girl he got pregnant," he said, "and about his son." He looked at MacKay. "I want to keep these, but we'll have copies made for your files."

MacKay nodded. "I understand. Let's see what's on the flash drive."

Morgan connected it into a port in his computer. When the monitor began displaying the contents, it showed a video of soldiers in the desert, obviously a location in Iraq. Jeff recognized Iraqi soldiers unloading crates from a US Military vehicle, while American soldiers stood and waited, weapons ready.

He had seen similar pictures on the SD card from Michael's camera. There were more videos. Different locations, but always the same American soldiers. Most of the pictures were not very clear because they were taken at night, with only the headlamps from the trucks lighting up the area.

Once, the camera zoomed in on a face. It was the face of John Parker. It was sharp enough to recognize his features.

"I believe we have enough to convict Parker," MacKay said.

"What about Larkin?" Jeff asked.

"Hard to say how guilty he is. We don't have much on him. He needs to be treated with kid gloves. He might be our next president."

* * * *

Jeff and Jenny went out for supper that evening to celebrate a small victory.

"I'm glad you finally know why your brother was murdered," she said.

He nodded, staring into his beer. "I don't know if I should be happy or angry. Whatever I feel, nothing will bring him back. He made many mistakes. One of them was getting an Iraqi girl pregnant, something hard to forgive since he was married to a wonderful woman. He tried his best to keep his conscience clear by sending money every month to the mother of his son, but in the end, her own people murdered her. One thing I don't understand is the fact he became involved in selling guns to our enemies."

Jenny shrugged. "Sometimes we get pulled into situations we have no control over. Remember, he was blackmailed by John Parker."

"I know. Obviously, it bothered him. There is over one hundred thousand dollars in an account. Money he never touched."

"He was not a bad guy, Jeff. You have to forgive him. He was your brother."

"He received a medal for bravery. They all did. For what? For betraying their country?"

"For fighting for their country. For defending freedom not only in America but for the whole world. None of those men was really bad, except for Parker."

"No, they weren't bad, just tainted," Jeff said with a bitter voice.

He phoned Detective Smith in Fresno the next day.

"I was wondering what happened to you, Jeff," Smith said. "It's been two weeks since the funeral."

"It's been two eventful weeks," Jeff said. "We've made some interesting discoveries and averted a major disaster. I can't tell you much on the phone, but I promise I'll tell you everything next time you and I get together. Which, hopefully, will be soon."

"Now you've made me curious. Have you found out who is behind the murders?" Smith came right down to the gist of it.

"Yes, we have."

There was a pause on Smith's end. "I'll be anxious to talk to you," he said at last.

Jeff could imagine that the young detective could barely contain himself, and he couldn't blame him. He had been trying all this time to put the puzzle together.

"We will talk soon, Marvin. Are you still holding Forester and Chandler?"

"Yes, we are. If you're asking have we contacted to police department in Sacramento, the answer is no. We will be trying those two men in Fresno, since this is where the murder occurred."

"I'm surprised to hear you still have them in custody. Didn't their lawyer ask for them to be released on bond?"

Smith chuckled. "Sure, he has, but the judge denied the request because of the severity of the case. He thinks they are a flight risk. The DA recommended it." He chuckled again. "Our DA is not crooked."

"You think the DA of Sacramento is?" Jeff asked.

"Well, he is married to the cousin of a mobster. Would you trust him?"

"I don't. He is one of the reasons I'm still on the run."

Rob came the next morning to pick him up. He was wearing his uniform. "I thought you might want to be present when we put Colonel O'Connor under arrest."

When Jeff slid into the backseat of Rob's car, he was surprised to see Colonel Cowley sitting in the passenger's seat, also in uniform.

"Hello, Lieutenant Chartrand."

"Hello, Colonel." Jeff noticed that he looked better than the last time he'd seen him. "You're looking good," he said.

"Why shouldn't I?" Cowley said. "It's a beautiful day. I'm finally going to see that bastard O'Connor get what he deserves and I'll be getting my job back."

"That's good to hear. I wish I could say he same," Jeff said.

"MacKay took you off the Most Wanted list," Cowley said.

"I'm still wanted for the murder of Galliano."

"They can't touch you," Cowley insisted. "You are still in the Armed Forces. You're not a civilian. If anyone will judge you, it will be a military court. I spoke to someone in Washington this morning. You are back in the system, officially, Lieutenant Chartrand. I've made it retroactive. You never left the Military." He smiled. "Even after the pension you've received in error all these years has been deducted from your back pay, you will still have a nice little sum left. It will take a few weeks until all the paperwork has been completed, just be patient."

Jeff was a little shocked when he heard the news. "You can do that?" he asked.

"You'd be surprised what can be done if you know the right people, Lieutenant," Cowley said.

Rob didn't talk much during the trip. He was busy maneuvering the car through the traffic. When they arrived at the military base, the rest of their team was already waiting by the gate.

The men saluted when they saw Colonel Cowley. They nodded to Jeff when he stepped out of the car.

The Colonel spoke to the guard at the gatehouse. Then they marched into the compound. Jeff noticed all of the men were dressed in military fatigues and they wore their sidearm. He felt somewhat out of place in his civilian garb.

The two guards outside Colonel O'Connor's office stood straight when they saw Cowley and his squad approaching.

"At ease," Colonel Cowley barked, and then he and his men walked into O'Connor's office.

O'Connor looked up, startled, when he saw the men filing in. "What is the meaning of this, Colonel?" he asked in a loud voice.

"Colonel James O'Connor, you are under arrest," Colonel Cowley said with an official sounding voice.

"What the hell are you talking about?" O'Connor bellowed. "You can't just barge into my office and arrest me! You have been decommissioned, Colonel Cowley."

"My position has been reinstated by General Farrell. As of this morning, I am the commanding Officer of this base and this office. You can confirm that by calling him in Washington. After you've been taken into custody." He turned to Rob. "Please, remove the Colonel from his post."

Rob walked up to O'Connor. "Please, don't give us any trouble, sir. I have my orders. Your sidearm, please."

O'Connor fumed visibly, but, after a moment's hesitation, he handed Rob his gun. "You will pay for this! All of you! I have friends in Washington."

"I doubt that, Colonel," Cowley said. "Not after the President reads the memo he receives from the National Security Council." Cowley allowed himself a small chuckle. "You've played your last game,

Colonel. Unfortunately, mine was the better hand."

After Rob and Harmon accompanied O'Connor out of the room, Colonel Cowley took his seat behind the desk.

Looking around the office, he said, "Ah, this feels good. I'll have to get rid of those awful pictures on the walls. That man has no taste." He looked at Jeff. "I've read Specialist Masters' report, Lieutenant. I want you and the team to fly to Norfolk and apprehend the men who are getting ready with a shipment of illegal weapons to Iraq. Intelligence reports a ship is being prepared to sail in two days. I have already been in contact with Colonel Settler and informed him of the situation. He will begin the investigation in Iraq and a sweep of the soldiers stationed there. The guilty ones will be caught and punished. You'll be met by a Captain Nelson in Norfolk."

"When do we leave, sir?" Jeff asked.

"Today. We can't waste any time."

"Can I make a call, Colonel?"

"Use my phone, Lieutenant."

"Thank you, sir."

Jeff dialed Morgan's number. "Morgan, can you tell Jenny I won't be coming home tonight. I'll be gone for a few days."

Morgan didn't ask for an explanation. He knew better. All he said, was, "Good luck, Lieutenant."

Jeff felt like being back in the old days. The cloak and dagger games were beginning again.

Rob and Harmon came back. "Ready, Colonel," Rob said. Obviously, he had already been briefed before he and Cowley picked up Jeff.

This time they took a military plane that would take the team to the airfield in Norfolk, Virginia. Jeff exchanged his civilian clothes for army fatigues. At least now he felt like one of the guys.

They arrived in Norfolk in the evening. When they walked out of the terminal, two uniformed men met them. "I'm Captain Nelson," one of them introduced himself. "We have a vehicle waiting for you."

The vehicle turned out to be a military truck. The team piled into it, and Jeff was surprised to find five men in black uniforms already sitting in the back. "I'm Lieutenant Mason," one of them said. "We are with Homeland Security. We'll be working together on this mission."

"Why weren't we told?" Jeff asked.

"Security." Mason shrugged. "The less people are involved in this, the less chance of it going wrong. We don't want to tip off anyone."

"All right, as long as it is understood this is our mission," Jeff said.

"Understood. We are here only to assist."

"I am Lieutenant Chartrand, by the way."

Mason smiled thinly. "I know. We've been briefed."

When they arrived at the harbor, Captain Nelson came up to Jeff. "I already put some of my men in position. The ship we want is that big freighter at the end, the *Ocean Maid*. I will go first and talk to the captain of the ship and I will tell him that he has to take on a squad of soldiers who will be accompanying him on a special mission to Iraq. There are a number of soldiers on board already, in addition to the regular crew, and they are considered hostiles."

"I understand. Thank you, Captain," Jeff said. "I notice that is not a US naval vessel."

"No. It's a private freighter on contract with the navy."

"I see." Jeff turned to his men. "We'll have to wait until Captain Nelson gives us the go-ahead."

They watched Nelson walking along the wharf toward the big ship. Jeff listened to the cries of the gulls and inhaled the ocean air, which was laced with the smell of fish, seaweed, and oil. The clanking of men and machines working on the anchored ships and on the waterfront seemed loud in his ears as he concentrated on his comm.

He saw Captain Nelson walking across the planks that connected the freighter to the shore. Through his binoculars, he watched as Nelson was approached by one of the seaman on board the big ship.

"I need to speak to your captain." Nelson's voice came clear over Jeff's comm.

"What's it about?"

"It's your captain's business," Nelson said sharply. "Take me to him immediately."

Jeff lost sight of the two men as they disappeared into the ship. Then he listened to the conversation that ensued between Nelson and the ship's captain.

"I wasn't informed of more men coming along," the captain said. "What happened to Lieutenant Sulvani?"

"He was detained," Nelson said. "From now on I'll be overseeing the operation."

"All right. Tell them to come aboard. I'll have someone show them to their quarters."

"Thank you, Captain Palmer. I'll let them know." He paused for a moment, then he said, "Permission to board granted. Go ahead."

Jeff had waited for the signal. "Let's go," he said.

He and his men started walking toward the ship. Lieutenant Mason and the four agents with him followed closely behind Jeff's team.

"Be alert," Jeff said with a low voice as they walked up the planks. To an observer it seemed as if they were armed only with handguns, which were strapped to their hips. He would have preferred M-16s, but holding machineguns openly would have aroused suspicion. Every man of his team carried a gym bag, apparently containing their possessions, when in reality each bag held a submachine gun. He hoped they wouldn't have to use them.

The team was met by a steward, who told them to follow him. He led them down a flight of stairs into the bowels of the ship. As soon as they were out of sight of any possible observer, Jeff told their guide to take them to the cargo hold. When he questioned Jeff's request, Jeff drew his gun, aimed it at the man's head and said, "Does this make it clear?"

"Very," the man said. Then he pointed ahead. "This will lead you to it."

"You just keep on walking," Jeff said. "And don't try to escape. You can't outrun a bullet."

"Who are you guys?" the steward asked. "If you're trying to hijack this ship, you should know there are quite a number of soldiers on board already. They may object to being kidnapped." He looked at the men behind Jeff. "You'll never get anywhere with your handguns."

"Don't worry your head about that," Jeff said. He turned to Rob and the others. "Show him your hardware."

They opened their gym bags and pulled out the machineguns. "Will this do?" Rob asked, grinning.

The man shrugged his shoulders. "Unless you're professionals, you'll never get off this ship alive."

"We don't intend to hijack this ship," Jeff said. "We just want to inspect your cargo, that's all. Now, move!"

They followed the steward down the corridor. When they came to the end, he said, "Through here."

"You first," Jeff said, watching him opening the door, ready to apprehend him should he decide to bolt and raise an alarm, but he just walked through the door and waited.

They were in a huge space filled with crates and other cargo. All of the crates were marked *Property of US Army.*

Jeff nodded to Armano, who nodded back. Then he grabbed the steward's arms and pinned them behind his back. Using a tie-wrap, he bound the man's hands together and proceeded to do the same to his feet.

"What should we do with him?" Armano asked.

"Stash him behind one of those crates," Jeff said. "Make sure he doesn't call out for help."

"All right, sir."

"Fan out and find the crates with the guns and ammunition," Jeff ordered the team. Then he said into his comm., "Captain Nelson, we are in the cargo hold. We need you to get the ship's manifest to let us compare the cargo with the records. I'll send some of my men to back you up. Wait for them." He looked at Mason. "Lieutenant Mason, take two of your men two the Captain's cabin and make sure the Captain doesn't decide to be a hero."

"Okay." Mason motioned to two of the agents and they left.

After a quick search, the team found a number of crates stacked with Rifles and ammunition, handguns and grenades. Some of them were unmarked. When they opened them, they discovered rocket launchers and rockets.

"I'm sure this crate is not on the manifest," Rob commented.

They counted the crates and estimated the number of rifles.

Jeff turned when he heard voices coming from the entrance to the cargo hold. It was Mason and his men. An elderly man wearing a captain's uniform struggled between the two agents, cursing loudly. Nelson walked slowly behind them.

Jeff waited until they were close. Then he said, "Good evening, Captain."

The Captain glared at him. "Are you in charge here?"

"Yes, I am."

"What is the meaning of this?"

"Just a routine inspection," Jeff said, calmly.

"Why wasn't I informed of that?" the Captain demanded. He turned and stared at Captain Nelson. "You, sir, came on board of my ship under false pretenses. And now I'm being held at gunpoint on my own ship."

"I apologize for the predicament you've been put in, Captain," Jeff said. "We have reason to believe some of the merchandise that has been loaded onto your ship is contraband. If your manifest agrees with the cargo then we are satisfied our information was wrong and you will be compensated for the inconvenience this has caused you."

"But, of course, you'll have to prove you were unaware of any discrepancies we may find," Mason injected. He handed Jeff a thick book. "The Captain believes in writing everything down neatly by hand. He doesn't trust computers."

"What kind of merchandise?" the Captain demanded to know.

"Guns, ammunition." Jeff shrugged. "Perhaps even a tank or two."

"I know nothing about that. I'm not the one keeping records." He sounded flustered and annoyed.

"But you're the captain of this ship. You should be aware of everything that happens on it," Jeff said. He turned to Rob. "Go ahead."

Rob took the book. He indicated Armano and Springer. "Let's go."

"We'll also need a list of all the men on board. Ship's personnel and the soldiers who are accompanying the cargo. I want to see passports and other identification."

The Captain stared angrily. "This is outrageous. I will file a complaint. Heads will roll, I'll promise you that."

"You have that prerogative," Jeff said. "Now, let us get on with our business."

Chapter Sixteen

It didn't take long to find discrepancies. Most of the shipment seemed to be on the up and up. Arms and ammunition destined for the troops in Iraq, but some of the orders were duplicates of other orders. Approved and signed by a Lieutenant Sulvani, who was stationed in Norfolk.

The Captain insisted he didn't know anything about those discrepancies.

"I have been dealing with the Military for many years. I wouldn't put that in jeopardy."

"We'll let a court decide, Captain," Jeff told him. "For now, consider yourself under arrest. Your ship will be impounded. The US navy will take over command and take it to Iraq on its scheduled run."

Jeff gathered his men and said, "There is no need to search the whole ship. We have enough evidence. We'll let others do the complete audit." He looked thoughtful. "This next phase of the operation will be the more difficult and dangerous one. We'll have to arrest the mercenaries and the soldiers involved in the smuggling of these weapons. In addition, all of the ship's officers have to undergo a thorough investigation. If at all possible, I want to avoid any bloodshed. Understood?"

The men nodded.

"Masters, I want you with me. The rest of you go on deck and await further instruction. Keep your weapons out of sight. Lieutenant Mason, you'll be in charge. Now, go!" Jeff spoke crisply.

When all the men had disappeared, he turned to the Captain. "You can make your case a lot easier if you cooperate, Captain Palmer."

"I told you I'm innocent of any crime. I promise you'll have my complete cooperation." The Captain seemed to have resigned to the situation. "I just want to get this over with as quickly as possible."

"So do we, Captain. Let's go to the bridge. I want you to tell all your officers, your personnel and everyone else to assemble on deck."

"All right."

As they walked past one of the crates, Jeff heard a noise and remembered the tied up steward. "Get him," he told Rob.

Rob went and brought the struggling man. He'd managed to spit out the cloth someone had stuffed into his mouth. Rob didn't remove the tie wrap from his arms, just from his legs to let him walk on his own.

The steward looked at the Captain and said, "Sorry, Captain Palmer, they overwhelmed me before I knew what was happening."

"It's okay," Captain Palmer said. "It's not your fault. I should have been more on the alert. Everything will be all right." He glared at Captain Nelson. "I was tricked."

Nelson shrugged but didn't comment.

Once they were on the bridge, the Captain followed Jeff's request. "This is the Captain speaking," he spoke into the intercom. "All officers, hands and passengers assemble on mid deck for inspection."

"Good," Jeff said. "Now, I want a list of every man and woman on board. Rob, you take it on deck and do a headcount. I want everyone accounted for."

"I don't have the information on the bridge," Captain Palmer said.

Jeff looked at the steward. "You take Masters and get the list." Then he said to Rob, "Shoot him if he tries to double-cross us."

Rob saluted and grabbed the man. "Let's go."

"And now we will join everyone on deck" Jeff said to the Captain.

Dusk was setting and someone turned on lights to flood the upper deck. Some of the personnel were already gathering. Jeff spotted a few men in uniforms. He looked for his team and discovered the men standing in the shadows. They didn't display any weapons, but they had their gym bags in front of them.

"Let's make ourselves visible," he told the Captain. Then he warned him, "No sudden moves, no warning remarks. Let it all happen peacefully."

Rob joined him and the Captain a few minutes later, carrying a long printout.

"Any trouble?" Jeff asked.

Rob shook his head. "None." Then he handed Jeff a bullhorn. "I thought you might need this."

Jeff smiled. "What would I do without you, Rob?"

He handed the bullhorn to Captain Palmer. "Here, you tell everyone to stay calm and not to resist. Tell them this is just a routine inspection. We want to see papers. Anyone who doesn't have them on their person, step over to the right. I'll have someone accompany them to their quarters to produce the papers. There will be no exceptions."

While the Captain spoke into the bullhorn, Jeff addressed his men over the comm. "Set up an inspection station and check everyone passing through. Make sure your weapons are visible this time. Keep a lookout for any potential trouble." Then he turned to the Captain. "Tell them to line up single file and follow my men's instructions."

Jeff watched as the small crowd reluctantly formed a line. A couple of Jeff's men told them how to proceed. He noticed a few people stepping aside. Most of them were ship's personnel. A couple wore uniforms. Jeff assumed those were the ones who didn't carry their papers on their person.

Rob had joined the team and given the men who did the checking the list he brought with him.

Things went rather smoothly, until one of the uniformed men bolted away and flung himself over the railing. When Jeff saw Springer following him, he said sharply, "Let him be. He won't get far. If he doesn't drown the coastguard will get him!"

The incident seemed to have stirred up more trouble. Jeff didn't see what happened, but he heard a gunshot. Someone shouted. When he looked, he saw a man on the ground, another one struggling with a third man. The man on the ground was dressed in black. One of Mason's agents. One man was running away.

Then Jeff saw another man in black aim his gun, fire it. The running man stumbled, caught himself. He made it to the railing, pulled himself onto it. The agent who fired the shot followed him at a run, but before he reached the fugitive, the man disappeared over the railing. The agent bent over the railing, and then he straightened and came back, shaking his head.

"The son of a bitch got away," Jeff heard him cursing over the comm.

In the meantime, the team had fanned out again, their M-16s in their hands, covering the agitated crowd.

Jeff took the bullhorn from the Captain's hands. "Everyone stay calm and get in line. If your papers are in order, you have nothing to fear. If they aren't, then give yourself up now and save everyone the unpleasantness of witnessing confrontations like this last one. You have nothing to gain by resisting."

"Who are you guys?" one of the soldiers yelled.

"I am Lieutenant Chartrand. With me are agents from Homeland Security. In case you're not aware of it, or haven't guessed by now, we are in the process of shutting down this operation. The people who are responsible for the trading of illegal arms have been apprehended. Any of you involved might as well resign to the fact you won't get paid from your employers, because they are already behind bars. Resist and you will only make your case worse."

He noted a few men in army fatigues stepping to one side. One of them talked to Hung and Armano. Then Jeff saw Lieutenant Mason bending over the man on the ground. He looked up and in Jeff's direction. "He needs medical attention. Ask the Captain if he has a medic on board."

Jeff turned to Captain Palmer. "Do you have a doctor on your ship?"

Captain Palmer nodded. "Give me the bullhorn." He took it and put it to his lips. "Doctor Mansfield. Attend to the injured man."

Jeff turned to Captain Nelson. "I think it is safe to bring in your men to accompany some of these people off the ship."

Nelson nodded. He pulled out his cell phone and called his people waiting close by. Soon the rumble of approaching army vehicles could be heard. Minutes later, armed soldiers swarmed on deck and took everyone in uniform, or appeared to be a military man, into custody. Some protested but gave it up when their protests were ignored.

The soldiers were quite efficient. It didn't take long until it was silent on board the freighters.

"What about me?" Captain Palmer asked. "I hope you won't put me in with all those common soldiers. Leave me some dignity."

"You'll come with me, sir," Captain Nelson said. "I promise you'll be treated with respect." He turned and saluted. "It was a pleasure to be of assistance, Lieutenant Chartrand."

Jeff saluted back. "Thanks for your help, Captain. Don't forget about Lieutenant Sulvani. He's the one who signed the papers."

Nelson smiled. "Don't worry. I've had my suspicions for some time about the Lieutenant and it will be a pleasure to finally get rid of him. To be honest, the man's been a pain in the ass ever since he was stationed here. Have a good trip home."

Jeff nodded and looked for his team. They had assembled not far from him and seemed to be waiting.

"It's finished, men," Jeff said into his comm. "Let's go home."

* * * *

Jeff decided to take a little side trip to Washington to find Tahir Uday, who had been bothering Barbara with his phone calls and threats. A trip that was a month overdue now. Since he was also the man who had ordered the weapons from Michael, this would not be just a personal trip. He would be able to justify it to Colonel Cowley.

While the rest of the team flew back to Sacramento, Jeff and Rob took a room in a motel. The next day, they went to a car rental agency and rented a car. It was only around one hundred forty miles to Washington. A three-hour trip. They made it there by noon.

Finding the address of Tahir Uday didn't take long. He lived in a swanky area of the city.

"This man lives well," Rob commented when they parked their car in the driveway of the two-story house.

"I wonder how much his job with the Embassy pays?" Jeff said.

"Not enough to afford a house like this, that's for sure," Rob said.

"I hope he's home. He should be, since it's Saturday." Jeff made sure his sidearm was secure in its holster. They hadn't bothered getting civilian clothes. It would be better if they wore army fatigues. They'd be allowed to display their guns openly without anyone asking questions.

They walked up the steps and rang the doorbell.

Someone inside approached the door, then it opened. Jeff stared at the bearded man standing in the open door.

He stared back at Jeff. "What are you doing here?" the man asked.

"Looking for you, Mr. Uday." Jeff chuckled. "I guess you're as surprised as I am. You didn't give me your name the last time we spoke, but I found you anyway."

"So you have, Mr. Chartrand. Have you come to pay me the twenty thousand dollars you owe me since your brother wasn't able to fulfill his contract?" The man seemed to have regained his composure. "We had to pay someone else to negotiate a deal with our business partners."

"Well, in case you haven't heard, there will be no more shipments, Mr. Uday. Your business partners are out of business."

"We'll find someone else," Uday smiled. "There are always those who are willing to deal."

Jeff stared at the smug visage of the man. "You are the man who is constantly harassing my sister. I want you to stop that and I want you out my family's life and out of mine. Forever. You are lucky I don't kill you for kidnapping my brother's son, but the guilty ones have been punished."

Uday's face turned ugly as he hissed at Jeff, "You are the one who murdered my brother when you rescued your brother's little bastard son. I pray to Allah some day he will grant that you will die by my sword!"

Jeff laughed. "Then you better pray real hard, Uday. Besides, if your brother was killed that night, then I know nothing about it. As far as I was concerned, there were only kidnappers and criminals present. We made sure they never kidnap innocent children again."

He put his face close to Uday. "Remember my words. If I ever hear your voice anywhere making threats toward me or my family, I will come and rip out your fucking throat and feed it to the dogs. Then I will cut your heart from your living body and watch you die. And don't count on joining your beloved Allah. You won't have died a hero's death in battle but a coward's death, because that's what you are. A fucking coward. All your so-called holy freedom fighters are. Anyone who blows himself up and murders innocent women and children is not a hero but a goddamned coward!"

Uday drew himself erect. "I am a warrior of Allah. You can't touch me. I have an Iraqi passport and I have diplomatic immunity."

"Fuck your diplomatic immunity, you son of a bitch. It won't protect you in my book. A dead man has never complained," Jeff snarled.

"I will not be intimidated, Mr. Chartrand. I know you won't follow through with your threat. After all, America is a civilized country and every man is treated equally." He allowed himself a smile. "You have laws you must adhere to and I am protected by your laws. If you break those laws, you will admit everything about America is a lie. No, I don't believe you will murder me in cold blood. In addition, Allah will protect me. Allah is great."

Jeff looked at Rob. "Do you believe this man? It just proves what I told you once, these people hide behind the very laws they despise so much."

He turned back to Uday. "Now, listen very carefully. You are right, we have laws and we follow them, but you are wrong about one thing and I'd like to make this perfectly clear to you. Even in this civilized country, there are some people who don't always stick to the law. I am one of them. And another thing you are wrong about...Allah will not be able to protect you if I decide to end your miserable life."

His words seemed to finally sink in. Uday's dark face looked gray under his beard. "I won't bother you again," he said, his accented voice thick and trembling.

Jeff relaxed. His anger abated slowly. "Let's go," he said to Rob, turning away. As they walked back to their car, some inner voice made him look back. When he turned his head and saw the gun in Uday's hand, he gave Rob a shove and dropped to the ground, drawing his own gun.

The sound of Uday's gun broke the silence. He heard the whining of the bullet as it missed him by inches, and then he fired his own weapon.

Just once.

Uday's body toppled over in slow motion. Jeff didn't wait to see if he was dead. "Let's get out of here," he said to Rob with urgency.

They got into their car and sped away.

"That bastard," Jeff cursed. "I didn't want to kill him. He left me no choice."

"I know," Rob said. "It was self-defense. I would have done the same."

"He was an Iraqi on American soil, but he was right when he said he was protected by diplomatic immunity." Jeff looked at the gun in his hand. "Fortunately, I didn't use my service revolver. I'll have to get rid of this gun."

Rob shrugged. "He deserved to die. Maybe it's better this way. One terrorist less in this world. Nobody cries."

Chapter Seventeen

Detective Smith finally decided to share his findings with the Sacramento police department. They arrested Dan Leighton and charged him with conspiracy to murder Connie Wu. He, of course, denied everything.

Jeff phoned Maxine and asked her to meet him at Barbara's house.

When she walked into Barbara's living room, Maxine gave him a friendly smile. Then she came up to him and kissed him on the cheek. "Good to see you, Jeff." She took a seat in the leather chair across from him. "You should turn yourself in, Jeff," she urged him.

Jeff shook his head. "Can't do. I don't trust the DA. He's married to Galliano's cousin, which means he will be biased. Besides, I am not a civilian anymore. I am a soldier and the Military has priority over a civilian court. Events that took place over the past weeks have brought about many changes, Maxine. I am no longer wanted by the FBI or the Department of Homeland Security. Those charges have been dropped."

She smiled. "When I said you should turn yourself in, I didn't mean that you would be taken into custody. It would be only a formality because they have nothing on you. They found a video camera in Galliano's office that taped the whole thing. Someone tried to suppress the tape, but I managed to get it released. It clearly shows you acted in self-defense."

"Well, that is good." Jeff breathed a sigh of relief. It seemed things were finally coming together in his favor.

"Captain Stoneman is wondering when you'll be coming back," Maxine said.

"I've thought about that," Jeff said. "I won't be coming back. Things won't be the same anymore. I've had an offer from Homeland Security, but I'm thinking of taking over the job of an old friend. He is getting on in years and his position is available. I've been promised a promotion to Colonel. It will mean a raise in my salary. It will also mean I'll be more or less stuck behind a desk, but I think I'm ready for it. I'm getting too old for all this action in the field."

Maxine gave him a warm smile. "I'm happy for you, Jeff. There is something else I need to tell you. It's about us."

Jeff had been dreading this. He felt guilty. He and Maxine had never really made any promises to each other, but his involvement with Jenny seemed to be more serious than he had thought at first. "Yes?"

"I don't know how to tell you this, Jeff. I mean, you and I, we had a good thing going." She seemed nervous, uneasy.

"Yes, we had," he said. "Still have."

"That's just it, Jeff. We had, but we don't anymore. What I want to say, I've met someone." She twiddled with a ring on her finger. When she noticed Jeff's eyes on it, she lifted her hand. "He gave me this."

"An engagement ring?" Jeff stared at the golden band with the sparkling stone.

"No, not an engagement ring. Just a ring."

"It looks expensive." He looked at her, questions in his expression. "Who?"

"Will Beacher."

"What?" Jeff didn't want to believe his ears. "Are we talking about Lieutenant Beacher from narcotics?"

"The very same." She smiled almost shyly.

"What the hell! He's too old for you."

She laughed. "He's forty-one. One year younger than you. Billy is very nice."

"I thought he was married."

"Divorced. His wife left him three years ago."

Jeff didn't know how to react to this news. He realized he was jealous. Which was totally ridicules. He should have been elated. This was the best thing that could have happened.

"I'm sorry," Maxine said. "It just happened. Sometimes we have no control over these things."

"I'm happy for you," he managed to say. "He is a good guy."

She stood up and joined him on the loveseat. Then she leaned against him. "What we had, you and I, it was special. I will always love you, but, like many beautiful things, it has come to an end. We can still be friends."

He pulled her to him and held her for a moment. "Yes, that we will always be. Friends. Friends who love each other."

* * * *

"The shares of United Oil are slowly moving back up on the stock market after taking a hit when CEO Herman Weinberg and members of the board of directors were arrested a month ago. They were charged with conspiracy to take control of the world's oil supply." The commentator looked at his colleague. "That's about it for today's stock market."

"Wow." The woman smiled. "Wasn't Senator Kenneth Osborne one of the major shareholders of UOC?"

"Yes, Olivia, he was. He has, of course, vehemently denied his involvement in the conspiracy. A spokesman for Senator Osborne says the Senator has no intentions of stepping down. Newcomer to the Senate, Senator Ronald Larkin, has also been implicated, but according to his lawyers, there is absolutely no truth to these ridiculous charges and he is planning to sue Homeland Security for slander."

Olivia smiled into the camera. Then she glanced at her male colleague. "If nothing else works, go into the offensive, right? That wouldn't be the first time a politician sues the government." She shuffled some papers. "And now to local news. Dan Leighton, the owner of The Three Palms Casino and brother-in-law of the late Joseph Galliano, has been found shot to death in front of his home. Police are not releasing any details, but according to confidential sources, his death seems gang related. Mr. Leighton's son, Jerry Leighton, suggests that he was assassinated by members of the Chicago mob in retaliation for the shooting of Mobster Anthony Mariano a few weeks ago..."

Jeff shut off the television.

He couldn't help but feel a measure of joy.

I guess Rob's remark to Mariano's secretary had its intended effect. Leighton got what he deserved. Too bad I didn't get a chance to ask him who gave the order to have Connie killed.

He looked at Agent MacKay. "After all the painstaking work we did the really guilty ones walk? How the hell is this possible?"

MacKay shrugged. "Politics."

"You know, I've been watching the news carefully every night. Not once have I heard anything about planned terrorist acts or assassination attempts on the President." Jeff shook his head. "Is the media so powerful they can suppress such news?"

"The media people only report what the government wants them to report. Certain people decided to put a lid on this whole thing for fear it might create panic among the population." MacKay said.

"Come on, MacKay. That's bullshit and you know it." Jeff didn't buy it. "Give the people more credit than that. Nobody panicked after 9/11. Sure, there were outcries and there was anger, but I didn't see any panic. We averted an attack and possibly saved the life of the President. Doesn't anyone get credit for that?"

MacKay chuckled. "How often have you and your team been involved in preventing exactly those same things, Chartrand? Maybe not as big but still important to the safety of this country?" He lifted a hand. "Don't answer that. It's just a rhetorical question. Did you ever get any credit for that? Did anyone?"

Jeff shrugged. "We did what we had to do."

"Exactly. And you and I will do so again. Ours is a job that never gets any thank-you-notes. Just knowing we did our job well has to be enough." He looked around the apartment and smiled. "I see you've redecorated. Sorry about the mess we left behind."

Jeff smirked. "I can't say I was happy with the way you treated my property, MacKay. I still don't see that it was necessary."

"Maybe it wasn't, but all indications implied you and your brother were involved in something concerning the security of our country. You have to admit, I was partially correct. Your brother was part of the arms smuggling ring."

"Yes, he was, but against his will."

"He took money."

"He never touched it. What happens to that money now?"

MacKay looked thoughtful, and then he shrugged. "Much of our investigation has been censored and some of the stuff we uncovered somehow got lost. I don't remember seeing any paperwork on any money. I would say if there is any money, it is yours. You understand?"

Jeff nodded. "I understand. By the way, thank you for that new computer."

MacKay smiled. "That was the least we could do to compensate you. I'm sorry you turned down my offer. We could use a man like you."

"I admit, I was tempted," Jeff said. "After throwing it around in my head for a while, I decided to accept Colonel Cowley's offer. His health is failing and he is retiring. I'll be taking over his position."

"Maybe we'll run into each other from time to time." MacKay smiled and rose. "Let's keep in touch, *Colonel* Chartrand."

"You already knew," Jeff said.

The agent nodded. "It's my business to know. See you around."

After MacKay left, Jeff got another beer, made himself comfortable on the couch and stared at the blank television screen. His thoughts began to wander and he was not happy.

The men who murdered Michael and his family had been apprehended and put behind bars. Mariano and Galliano, who gave the order for the murders, were dead, as was Colonel O'Connor, who committed suicide. His brother Harry O'Connor and Herman Weinberg were still on trial and might just walk away as free men.

Senator Osborne and Ronald Larkin would probably never go to trial. Larkin might even end up being the next President of the United States.

American Defense Manufacturing was under investigation, but according to MacKay, nothing had been found yet to implicate the company. The FBI arrested Paul Clark and a few other employees of ADM.

One good thing came out of it. The Military had quietly rooted out a number of soldiers and officers who were involved in the selling of weapons, but Jeff knew, it wouldn't stop the illegal arms deals. Somebody else would fill the void. Nothing would change.

When he heard the knock on the door, he went and opened it.

"Hi, Jenny," he said.

She came into his arms and kissed him. "Hi, Jeff." She looked at the bottle in his hand. "I see you're having an affair with someone else. Did you miss me?"

He smiled. "I always miss you when you're not with me."

"How about a beer?" she asked, sitting down on the couch.

"Sure." He went to the fridge and got her a bottle. "Have you been watching the news?"

She nodded. "I have. You must be disappointed. I also have some news you may not like."

"You have?" He sat down beside her. "Are you going to tell me you've found someone else?"

"No, silly. You are the only one." She put her finger on his nose. "I love you too much to even look at another man." She became serious. "My father has a new client. Guess who?"

"I have no idea."

"John Parker."

"What!" Jeff sat up and stared at her. "Tell me you're joking."

"I wish I were. I knew you'd be upset."

"That son of a bitch had my brother and his family killed. He is responsible for the death of a woman I cared for and the murder of my brother's friends. Why would your father even think about defending a man like that?"

Jenny shrugged. "My father asked me to be present when Parker came in. He told him I was his secretary. Parker claims he is innocent of most of the charges. He admits to dealing in weapons, but he denies his involvement in the murders. Those videos that were taken when that Iraqi girl was raped and murdered? They never showed any faces, remember?"

"We have Michael's and McGee's written statements," Jeff said.

"He claims that everyone in his unit was so drunk that night, nobody really remembers anything clearly." She paused and studied his face. "Now here it becomes weird. He says the event went down differently from Michael and McGee's version. According to him, he was the one who raped the Iraqi girl and Ronald Larkin shot her. The next day, Larkin told his men Parker committed the murder."

"That whole story sounds pretty farfetched, don't you agree?"

"Well, there is one thing that supplies food for thought. It was Parker's birthday that day, not Larkin's. I checked it out."

"Next thing you'll tell me Parker didn't shoot John MacKay and Darrin Montana either?"

"Well, he says it's true MacKay was shot by friendly fire, but it wasn't his gun that killed him. He was in front of MacKay when it happened, which means he couldn't have been the shooter."

"What about Montana?"

"There again, he claims it happened the way he reported the incident. Darrin Montana was shot by insurgents. There are no witnesses who can say otherwise. Everything is pure speculation." Jenny took a sip from her bottle. Then she leaned against him. "Things are not always what they seem. People have selective, sometimes false, memories."

Jeff sat beside her, silent, his eyes staring blindly, seeing nothing.

Could there be any truth to what Parker claimed? Obviously, he would protect his commanding officer and friend Larkin, especially since he might get a shot at the Whitehouse. Being Larkin's right hand man would give him status and power, but it seemed Larkin threw him to the wolves. Now Parker was fighting back. He had nothing to lose.

"What do you think?" he asked.

"Well, I am not as close to it than you are, Jeff, and not as biased.

I'd say there could be some truth to what Parker claims. My father shares my belief." Her eyes looked thoughtful. "Parker gave us another name. Colonel Montgomery. He is a CIA operative and he is one of the people who gave Parker his orders."

"One of the people?" Jeff asked. "How many more are there?"

She shrugged. "We will never really know. Apparently, it goes way up. People close to the President are involved...people the President trusts with his life. Just think about it for a moment, Jeff. John Parker isn't smart enough to have planned this whole thing by himself. He was only another puppet...as he claims. Not innocent, mind you, but he was not the puppet master."

Jeff stared at the plagues on the wall. The Purple Heart was his. He had finally taken it out of his closet. The other medal belonged to Michael. Medals of Honor. All the men in Michael's unit had received them. Awarded for exceptional valor.

Jeff looked at them with bitterness.

Tarnished Valor.

The End

www.ingramcontent.com/pod-product-compliance
Lightning Source LLC
Chambersburg PA
CBHW020127180626
46810CB00004B/1441